HAND OF GOD

DEFIANCE #2

JASON KRUMBINE

Published by Lantern Key Books

ISBN: 978-1-971197-01-2

Originally published in 2018 by Jason Krumbine.

First Lantern Key Books Edition: December 2025

about this book

On the edge of UPA space a mysterious vessel has appeared.

No one knows where it came from.

It has no callsign or identifying marks.

The vessel simply transmits a standard S.O.S. in a signal that hasn't been used in hundreds of years: Morse code.

While still recovering from their losses on Carlock, the USS Defiance is dispatched to investigate. But when they arrive they discover that every single individual on the ship has already been dead for hundreds of years.

As Captain Mitchell and his crew work to unravel the mystery of this ghost ship, they soon find themselves confronted by something far worse than a simple space mystery:

What killed this crew so long ago is still very much onboard and still is very much alive.

Books in the Defiance Series

Defiance
Hand of God
Act of God
The Test of Truth
The Price of Paradise
The Value of Terror
The Last Breath of a Dying Tomorrow

Subscribe to my newsletter and I'll let you know as soon as the next Defiance book is ready to read.

https://onestrayword.beehiiv.com/subscribe

HAND OF GOD

One hundred years ago the United Planetary Alliance was attacked by a parasitic, single-minded species from another dimension that consumes and absorbs everyone and everything it comes into contact with. Today this species is known as the Unity. After this initial attack, the Unity was never heard from again.

The Veneer Empire was a former member of the UPA until the Unity's attack. In the aftermath, they withdrew from the UPA and reestablished borders that hadn't been used in hundreds of years. No one has heard from the Veneer since.

Today, Captain Gavin Mitchell commands the USS Defiance, an eighty-year-old starship that was built as a response to the threat of the Unity. The Defiance is currently based out of Starbase Atlantic where it patrols a region of space that is largely removed from regular UPA presence.

Captain Mitchell is also, secretly, under the command of Admiral Philip Wanamaker and Directive 52, which is responsible for protecting the UPA from threats too dangerous for the public to know. Directive 52 operates at the upper echelons of the top-secret community and works independently within the governing body of the UPA.

Starbase Atlantic is currently under the command of Commodore Kathryn Straub, Mitchell's former first officer from an earlier command.

President D'Ambra is the duly elected leader of the United Planetary Alliance. He believes in full transparency and peace at all costs. His administration believes the Unity is no longer a threat and is nothing more than a boogeyman invented by the military complex and espionage community to further their own agendas.

Recently the Defiance was dispatched to investigate a potential Unity incursion on the planet Carlock. What they found was a previously uncharted stable wormhole and a secret Veneer base located on the planet. It was discovered that Veneer were using this wormhole as a secret backdoor in and out of Veneer space in order to maintain this secret base. It was also discovered that the reason that the UPA hadn't heard from the Unity in the last one hundred years is because the Unity is unable to survive within our dimension. For reasons currently unknown, the Unity and the Veneer established an alliance decades ago in an attempt to solve this problem.

During their encounter with the Unity, the first officer of the Defiance, Commander Grace Hawkins, was killed and absorbed into the Unity.

During the attack Ensign Erin Calloway was engaged by the Unity. She and the Unity communicated in a language unfamiliar to anyone in this reality. Ensign Calloway is currently unaware of this encounter.

With the death of Commander Hawkins, the D'Ambra administration is attempting to install a new first officer whose loyalty would lie with President D'Ambra before Captain Mitchell.

Unbeknownst to everyone, however, in the aftermath of the Defiance's encounter with the Unity something changed and for the first time in one hundred years, the Unity has a stable presence in our reality.

1

STARBASE ATLANTIC

KATHRYN STRAUB's head had already hit the pillow. Her eyes were closed long before that. From the moment she sat down on her bed, her brain had begun the process of disconnecting from its conscious state.

In all fairness, though, she had begun the process even before she had even made it to her quarters. It had been a long day made unnecessarily longer by bureaucrats she wasn't allowed to punch. Not that there were any bureaucrats she was allowed to punch, officially.

Unofficially, the Vaul considered it to be an offense of the highest order if every political transaction didn't start with a fist to the face. How long had it been since she had dealt with a Vaulian? Six years? Longer? Those were the good old days…

That was the last thought that drifted through her head as she gave in to the exhaustion that she had been fighting with for the last eighteen hours.

Straub's eyes closed. Her head hit the pillow and she completely let go.

And then her comm went off.

"Son of a bitch," she muttered into her pillow. She grabbed her other pillow and pressed it over her head, hoping to drown out the incessant chirp of the comm. Eventually whoever it was would give up.

Except, it didn't normally take this long.

Her comm continued to chirp away, refusing to give her a moment's peace.

Straub sat up, violently throwing the pillow that had been covering her head across the room. "*Son of a bitch!*" she shouted again and this time it was followed by a string of curses in no less than three different languages.

Of course, she was alone in her quarters, so there wasn't anyone there to truly appreciate how adept she was at swearing in three different alien tongues. Four, if you counted her native English.

Straub smacked the small touchscreen on her night-stand that was flashing with the communications icon. "I haven't had more than three hours of sleep in the last three days. I left explicit orders not to be disturbed for the next six hours. So whoever the hell you are, you better have a damn good reason for bothering me right now. I swear, if we're not under attack or President D'Ambra himself isn't about to set foot on this station, I will find the most *remote* outpost in the UPA, and I mean the kind of place that makes the middle of nowhere look crowded. This place is going to be so remote that it'll take *weeks* for a subspace signal to reach you. You won't even have a plant to talk to. It'll be dust or ice. Miles and miles of dust or ice. And you won't get so lucky that it'll be dust *and* ice. No. It'll defi-nitely be one or the other. I will find this desolate outpost and I will make sure that you're stationed there until your dying day. And then, I'll make sure, after you're dead, you'll be *buried* there. So that, even in death, you'll be stuck out in the asshole of the galaxy." Straub paused to take a deep breath. "With that in mind, who are you and why are you calling me?"

There was a long pause on the other end of the comm. Long enough that Straub had to double check to make sure the channel was still even open.

"Hello?" Straub asked.

"Ensign Ogletree can't come to the phone right now on a count of the fact you just made him piss himself into a panic attack."

Straub recognized the voice immediately. Lieutenant Commander Marv Mallozzi. Third shift command officer.

Straub sighed and rubbed her face. "Damnit, Marv."

"Yeah, well, it's not like I was looking forward to waking you either," he said. "I heard about what happened with the ambassadors from Struqoid and Aurrod earlier today."

Straub groaned loudly and dropped her face into her hands.

"You know, considering how big a station we are, it's remarkable how fast information travels around here," Mallozzi continued. "Personally, I would have been more than content to not speak with you for another week. By my calculations, I figured that should be enough time for you clear out all of your pent-up hostility. But, hey, it turns out that's no longer a problem. Of course, Ensign Ogletree here is going to be suffering with the lingering embarrassment of pissing himself while on duty and most likely a lifetime's worth of post-traumatic stress disorders."

"Son of a bitch," Straub muttered.

"I'd rather not talk about my mother right now, ma'am," Mallozzi said. "I think it's probably enough to drive one officer to tears for now."

She glared up at the ceiling in the direction of the command deck. "Is there a reason you're calling me right now? Or did you just want to try out some of your new smart ass material?"

"Ensign Ogletree was calling you because we just received an interesting signal from a sensor buoy we have in the Uslen system."

"It better be damn interesting, Marv." Straub didn't make any move to get out of her bed.

"Are you familiar with Morse code?"

Straub rubbed her tired eyes, searching her exhausted brain. "That sounds familiar."

"It's an old Earth method of transmitting information," Mallozzi said. "According to the computer, it hasn't been used in almost four hundred years."

"A history lesson is not worth waking me up," Straub said.

"It's not a history lesson, ma'am," Mallozzi said. "That's what our buoy's picking up out there. Somebody's transmitting a distress signal in Morse code."

2

THE *ATLANTIC'S* command deck was centrally located. Buried deep in the starbase, it was only three decks up from main engineering and two decks down from the all-purpose storage spaces primarily used for docked ships. It was a large dual-level circular room with wide viewscreens that wrapped around the entire circumference.

When Straub stepped off the lift, she paused for a moment, letting her eyes adjust to the dim lighting of the third shift. She mumbled a Sweezakaal swear under her breath as she made her way down the handful of stairs to the command table where a lanky man with unusually long limbs and a perpetually furrowed brow stood.

"The least you could have done is turn up the damn lights," Straub grumbled. Her uniform had a rumpled appearance and, in fact, had actually been fished out of her dirty laundry. Her gray hair was pulled back into a simple ponytail and she held a cup of Elwat spice coffee in her left hand.

"Well, I figured that you were already pissed off," Mallozzi replied, looking up from the command table. "So I

didn't really see the point in upsetting my shift any further."
He was an Aztix. In addition to his long limbs, his skin had
a vaguely blue tint to it that was almost imperceptible in the
dim lighting of the command deck. His face was long with
narrow eyes that extended up towards his forehead and a
flat nose. His lips were deceptively small, giving the impression that the rest of his mouth was as well. However, his jaw
was double jointed and the sight of him eating made most
of his crewmates intensely uncomfortable.

Straub glared at him and took a sip from her coffee.
The jolt from the Elwat caffeine made her toes curl.

Mallozzi wrinkled his nose in disgust. "I don't know
how you can drink that stuff."

Straub set the cup down. "It's the only thing keeping
me upright now."

"I suggest you go see Doc Hogle," Mallozzi said. "But
I'm afraid that would set off a series of unfortunate events
once they realize your blood has been replaced by that
disgusting flavored cup of Elwat spices you call coffee."

Straub leaned forward, propping her hands against the
table and looked her second-in-command right in the eyes.
"I want you to listen to me very carefully. Are you
listening?"

"With bated breath."

"You're not as funny as you think you are."

Mallozzi shrugged his slender shoulders and turned his
attention back to the screens on the table. "Did you
happen to spot a wet, balled up uniform on your way in?"

"No, why?"

"No reason. It's just what's left of Ensign Ogletree," he
replied. "I thought you might want to get a good look at
him before somebody rolls him onto the next ship bound
for Earth."

"You're an asshole."

"You know how long he's been here?" Mallozzi held up three long fingers. "I'll save you the trouble. Three weeks. That's a new record for you."

Straub took another sip from her coffee and waited for the little caffeine jolt before she replied. "You know, you were the one who had him call me."

Mallozzi nodded. "True enough. That was an unfortunate miscalculation on my part."

She eyed him. "Was it, though?"

"I understand what you're attempting to suggest, but I'll have you know, I was planning on taking Ensign Ogletree under my wing. I was going to mentor him."

"Uh-huh." Straub didn't sound convinced. "Pass along your invaluable wisdom?"

"That was the plan."

"Like how you ended up as third shift commander on a remote starbase next door the Veneer Empire?"

"We all have humble beginnings."

Straub tugged at her collar uncomfortably. "What the hell's wrong with the temperature in here? Feels like I walked into a damn sauna."

"I've spoken with engineering about it. They're working on it. Honestly, though, I found it too be rather refreshing," Mallozzi said. "So I told them not to rush it. Of course, this was before I realized I was going to have to endure your presence this evening."

Straub lowered the zipper from her neckline to just under her collarbone. "You know, I could find a worse assignment for you around here."

"I'm sure you can."

"Somebody needs to clean the toilets."

"Nobody will ever accuse you of favoritism."

She twirled an impatient figure at the screens. "What's going on?"

Mallozzi shrugged. "I wish I knew."

"It's a distress signal," Straub said. "When I asked what's going on, I already know. What I'm really asking for are the *details*."

Mallozzie continued, unperturbed. "The first portion of the signal is a standard S.O.S. No ship identification or callsign. Just a boilerplate distress signal. It's literally S-O-S."

"Sometimes the classics are still the best."

"Naturally," Mallozzi agreed. "Except the transmission is over eighty petabytes."

Straub frowned. "What's the rest of it?"

Mallozzi shrugged. "I don't know. It has the computer…discombobulated"

"You said it was Morse code," Straub replied. "And the computer can't translate it? What the hell's wrong with the computer."

"Nothing. The problem's not with the computer." He gestured to the data on the screen closest to Straub. "The problem is with the code. It translates into pure gibberish."

"The hell?" Straub scrolled through the information. "What is this even supposed to be?"

"I'm pretty sure 'gibberish' covered it."

"What else is out there?"

"According to the buoy, nothing," Mallozzi said. "Just our mysterious vessel and their equally mysterious distress signal in Morse code.

Straub took another sip from her coffee. "I'm going to need something stronger for this."

Mallozzi raised both of his eyebrows. "Well, you may want to wait a moment before breaking out M'reth ale.

After I got off the comm with you, we downloaded another update from the buoy before it went dark."

"Son of a bitch," she muttered. "What happened to it?"

Mallozzi shrugged. "It just went offline. Maybe it lost power. Maybe something blasted it."

"Did it look like something blasted it?"

Mallozzi didn't respond. Instead, he pursed his lips together and transferred another batch of data to her screen. This one included a video file.

It was a short video. Only thirty seconds. But Straub didn't need to see more than ten.

"Son of a bitch," she whispered. She looked up around the command deck, checking to see who was on duty, before returning her gaze back to Mallozzi. "Who else has seen this?"

"You and me," Mallozzi said. "After Ogletree I didn't think it was fair to subject you to anyone else tonight."

Straub hit replay on the video. "Who's in the area?"

"The *Perry's* three hours out," Mallozzi said.

"Yeah?"

"But I figured you'd probably want the *Defiance*," he added.

"How much farther?"

"Not much. At max speed, maybe three and a half hours. Four at the most."

Straub inhaled and then exhaled slowly, puffing her cheeks out as she watched, for a third time, a familiar wormhole open up and an unidentified ship exit it.

"Alright," she said. "Get me Mitchell on a secured channel."

3

USS DEFIANCE

THE WAILING WOULDN'T STOP.

It was a plaintive, almost desperate wail that just seemed to echo through everything: furniture, pillows, walls. Nothing seemed to stop the wailing. Instead of providing an obstacle, these things seemed to strengthen the wail, to give it sustenance, power.

And so, the wailing went on.

And on.

And on.

It was *endless*.

Nobody, in the entire galaxy, should be able to wail for that long.

And yet...

Lieutenant Commander Sadie Sadler lifted her head from her pathetic excuse for a pillow and glanced at the time on her nightstand. Despite what it felt like, the wailing had only been going on for a few minutes. Five to be exact.

Five minutes.

Five whole minutes.

She dropped her head back on to the pillow face first

and groaned loudly. But, she could barely hear herself over the wailing.

Five entire minutes.

It felt like *hours*. But it had only been five minutes. It was going to be hours, because it always ended up being hours. But now, after feeling like it had been hours after only five minutes, what was it going to feel like after several hours?

She rolled over onto her back and stared up at the ceiling. "This is what torture feels like," Sadler said out loud to her empty room. "This is real, genuine, torture. And this is how I'm going to die."

As if in response, the wailing became louder and more high-pitched.

Sadler squeezed her eyes shut. It felt as though the wail was physically stabbing her brain, and then dragging hot coals across the gray matter that so desperately wanted nothing more than to sleep.

Finally, in a fit of desperation, Sadler jumped out of her bed, grabbing her robe as she went, and stomped out into the cramped hallway of deck three. "I'm going to kill him," she muttered to herself.

A passing ensign stopped abruptly as Sadler bolted out of her quarters, muttering vague threats and stared at her.

Sadie Sadler was a petite woman with short blonde hair and was generally considered one of, if not the most, optimistic and upbeat officer on the *Defiance*. She was slow to speak ill of anyone and was quick to always point out that the proverbial glass was half full rather than half empty.

However, everyone has their off days.

Sadler cinched the belt of her robe tight and gave the ensign a narrow look "What the hell are you looking at?"

The ensign swallowed nervously and made an attempt to look anywhere but at her. "N-N-Nothing, ma'am."

"Then I strongly suggest you go look at it elsewhere," Sadler snapped.

The ensign bobbed his head in agreement and made for the nearest lift as fast as he could.

Sadler turned to her right and took three quick steps to the door of her neighbor.

Out in the corridor, remarkably, the wailing was muffled.

Not muffled enough that Sadler would consider attempting to sleep out in the corridor. But it was dialed back to the point where she didn't feel it rattling her back molars.

"I'm definitely going to kill him," she repeated. "Definitely ."

She didn't bother with the politeness of tapping the small touchscreen at the side of the door that would set off a gentle alert on the other side allowing the occupant to know there was somebody waiting for them.

Instead, Sadler pounded on the door with her fist.

Alarmingly, the door actually rattled quite a bit under her tiny fist.

Sadler stopped and took half a step back, making a mental note to check with Chief Engineer Warrick on whether or not the doors on the *Defiance* should be so easily rattled.

Before she had the opportunity to weigh the potential consequences of pounding on the door again, it slid open, revealing a naked orange man on the other side.

Lt. Commander Kinlin Nax, like all Natuzzi men, was completely hairless. His orange skin had a permanent sheen to it that most people, under certain lighting condi-tions, mistook for sweat. But Natuzzi did not sweat. Nor did they cry or have any saliva or urge to spit. They were a uniquely dry species.

The Natuzzi as a whole also had very little in the way of personal space or what most other races would consider personal 'barriers.' As such, this was not the first time, nor would it be the last, Kinlin Nax would forget to clothe himself before answering the door of his personal quarters.

For a moment, Sadler forgot what she was doing out here as her gaze naturally drifted south.

She grabbed both sides of her face and shook it, turning her focus upwards towards the naked man's face.

"Yes, Commander? Can I help you?" Nax asked.

"Can you help me?" Sadler repeated. "Can *you* help *me*?" Her high-pitched voice had a frantic edge to it that that was sharpened to a point by her southern twang. "*Can you help me?*"

Standing there in the cramped corridor of deck three Sadler trembled before the naked orange man with barely controlled rage, her face almost turning red.

"Can. You. *Help. Me?*" she repeated again.

Nax frowned. "You seem…upset."

Sadler's hands clutched at the air between them, like she wanted to violently choke something. "Do you have any gorram idea what *time* it is?"

Nax raised a hairless eyebrow and didn't say anything for a moment. Then, raising his voice slightly, he asked, "Computer, what's the current time?"

"The time is zero-two-hundred hours," the computer replied.

"Is there anything else I can assist you with, Commander?" Nax asked.

"I'm going to kill you," she said.

Both of Nax's eyebrows went up. "I think it would be better if that was something I stayed out of," he replied.

"Additionally, I'm inclined to voice my protest to the notion."

"*Protest?*" Sadler snapped. She pushed her fingers through her blonde hair in an effort to keep herself from strangling the Natuzzi. "Do you have any idea what my life has been like for the last three weeks? Not only do I have to manage all of my regular duties as nightshift commander around here, but I also get to be the acting first officer until we get a replacement. I am literally working *two* damn jobs. That's twice as many as you have to do. Which means, I get even less sleep than I normally would. And what little sleep I have been able to squeeze in, is usually interrupted by the *wailing*. The gorram *endless wailing* from your quarters. It *never* stops. I *beg* for it to stop, but it *doesn't*. Nax, I haven't had more than a couple of hours of sleep every night for the last two weeks." She pointed at her temple. "I can't even think straight anymore. I'm seriously considering straight up murdering you and I'm so sleep deprived, I can't actually figure out if that's a bad idea or not."

"I think it's safe to say it's a bad idea," he replied evenly.

"I'm not so certain right now," Sadler replied through gritted teeth.

"Commander, it occurs to me that perhaps I need to remind you the reason that you're currently filling two roles on this ship," Nax said, his voice never wavering.

Immediately, some of the wind left Sadler's sails. She visibly deflated and her shoulders sagged. "Ah, damnit." She rubbed her forehead and sighed. "I'm sorry."

"I understand you're having a difficult time right now," Nax continued. "But I too have been affected by the passing of our former first commander."

Sadler frowned, folding her arms. "There is literally no

one on this ship that didn't know you and Grace were hooking up. I think it's safe to use her name."

"I'm attempting to maintain some sense of decorum," Nax replied.

Sadler gestured at his naked body. "I think it's safe to say that ship has already sailed.

Nax looked down, as if taking notice of his lack of clothing for the first time. "Ah. Yes. I can see how this might be considered unprofessional. Please excuse me for a moment." He stepped back into his quarters, leaving the door open.

Suddenly, Sadler felt a little conspicuous standing in the empty corridor. She pulled her robe a little tighter and thought about how the meeting would go when the captain wanted to know why she was spotted rampaging through the corridor of deck three, pounding on doors.

She cleared her throat. "Mind if I step inside? It just occurred to me that the acting first officer probably shouldn't be seen running around in her robe."

"Please," Nax replied from his bedroom. "Make yourself at home, Commander."

"We're off duty," Sadler said, stepping into his quarters. "It's Sadie."

Nax's quarters were basically the same as hers, except everything was laid out in the reverse. Somehow, though, it seemed smaller. The walls were covered in thick rugs that had intricate patterns of silver woven into them. There was a slight breeze from the ventilation system and the rugs swayed. As they moved, the silver patterns appeared to change shape. She took a step towards one of them for a closer look when Nax came out of his bedroom, now clothed in a loose fitting outfit.

Sadler took a step back towards the center of the room.

"Sorry. Didn't mean to be nosy." She nodded at the rugs. "They're pretty."

Nax nodded. "Yes they are."

"What are they?"

"Grace's," Nax replied. Again, his voice was even, calm, as though they were simply discussing the day's agenda.

"Ah. I'm sorry," Sadler replied. She looked around his quarters, suddenly feeling awkward.

"There's nothing to apologize for, Commander."

"Sadie," she corrected him.

He tilted his head towards her for a moment. "Sadie." He clasped his hands behind his back as they studied the rugs. "These are ceremonial M'reth prayer rugs. Grace collected them."

Now it was Sadler's turn to raise her eyebrows. "Seriously?"

Nax shrugged. "I didn't understand it myself."

"Don't the M'reth make what's considered some of the most beautiful and breathtaking jewelry in the galaxy?"

"That they do."

"And Grace collected their *prayer rugs*?"

"There is a human phrase that Warrick taught me," Nax said. "I've clung to it ever since I first heard it. As the only Natuzzi in the Fleet, it has helped me tremendously as I have navigated my way through the Alliance, meeting new species and making new acquaintants."

"Oh? What is the magical bit of wisdom that Warrick imparted to you?"

"There is no accounting for taste."

Sadler burst out laughing.

"I'm sorry," she said after a minute. "That wasn't appropriate." She giggled. "Neither was that. I'm really sleep deprived.

Nax smiled. "No, you're right. It's funny."

Sadler wiped tears from her eyes and took a deep breath to calm herself down from the giggles. "Seriously, Nax, what the hell is going on?"

"I'm not quite sure I understand."

She gestured towards his bedroom which shared an adjoining wall with her own. "I hear you every night. Endless wailing. Hell, half the deck has to hear you."

Nax focused his gaze on the prayer rugs. "As you pointed out, Grace Hawkins and I were romantically involved."

"That's a….diplomatic way of putting it," Sadler said.

Nax shrugged. "While we never took the time the clarify the exact nature of our relationship, it's safe to say that I developed rather intense feelings for her."

She stared at him for a moment. "Are you trying to say that the two of you were in love?"

Nax shrugged again.

Sadler sighed again, rubbing her eyes. "Nax, I haven't gotten any sleep because of the wailing."

"It is an ancient Natuzzi grieving ritual," Nax replied. "You have my sincerest apologies if it has been disturbing you."

"Well, that'll certainly make up for the parts of my brain that are feeding on each other," she muttered. Sadler shook her head and looked at Nax. "Wait a minute. I thought y'all didn't believe anyone actually died?"

"As I said," Nax replied. "It is an *ancient* ritual."

Sadler raised an eyebrow.

"I am doing the best I can, Commander," Nax said. "This is an unfamiliar situation I find myself in. As you pointed out, my people don't believe in death. But, Grace Hawkins was not a Natuzzi and as I'm sure Warrick has already explained to you, our beliefs cannot be applied to anyone who is not Natuzzi."

Sadler rubbed her hands along her arms. "Yeah, he may have mentioned something about the rest of the galaxy not counting in the general Natuzzi belief systems."

Nax raised his hands, palms up. "We are a complicated species."

"The Ovvin can only reproduce every thirty years. *That's* complicated. You people..." She trailed off, not entirely certain how to put her feelings into words.

"As I said, it's an ancient ritual," Nax said. "We weren't always this way."

Sadler exhaled, puffing out her cheeks. "Well, have you considered that you ended up this way because your ancient grieving ritual involved too much endless wailing?" She held up a hand to stop him from responding. "Don't bother. That was out of line. Have I mentioned that I'm sleep deprived?"

"As am I. I don't believe I've slept since Grace's passing."

Sadler stared at him. "Nax, that was almost five weeks ago."

He clasped his hands behind his back again. "Indeed it was."

Neither of them spoke for a few minutes.

Sadler wasn't sure what to say. Something needed to be said, but she couldn't quite figure out what it was. She watched the patterns on the M'reth prayer rugs shift in the gentle breeze from the ventilation system.

Finally, Nax said, "Ms. Sadler-"

"Sadie."

"Sadie," Nax corrected himself. "The M'reth believe that when we die, we are all reborn in a parallel dimension where we then exist in a form that is the direct opposite of what we had when we were living."

"I…" She looked at him. "Seriously?"

Nax nodded. "I have been searching for something, but I do not know what it is. To my people, death is a simple balancing of the universal scales in an effort to achieve universal harmony. We don't believe in an afterlife. We do, believe, however, that there is a purpose to our *being*. But those who are not of Natuzzi, have no purpose. That would mean that Grace has," he paused to correct himself, "*had* no purpose. I don't know what to make of this. I never imagined myself in this scenario." He took a deep breath. "Warrick believes that when we die, we simply cease to exist." Nax snapped his fingers. "Just like that. As far as he is concerned, this is all there is and once it is over…" Nax shrugged. "There's nothing."

"That's a depressing point of view," Sadler said.

"But is it any different than that of my people?"

"Well, I mean," Sadler stumbled for a moment.

Nax looked at her. "As I understand it, your parents are missionaries for the Evangelical Church of Christ. You must have some unique insights on what happens after death."

"Well, ah." Sadler gave a humorless laugh. "I don't know that I'm the person you want to be looking for after-life advice from."

"And why is that?"

Sadler stretched her neck to the side, cracking it. "You might say that I'm a lapsed Christian. I don't exactly see eye-to-eye with my parent's take on how the universe works."

"You maintain a relatively close relationship with your mother."

"Well sure," Sadler said. "It's great. As long as we don't talk about anything important."

"But surely, despite this, you must have some belief of what is to come after we die?" Nax asked.

Sadler shrugged. "Honestly, I don't like to give it much thought. Death isn't exactly a cheerful topic."

"But it comes for us all eventually."

"That doesn't mean I want to dwell on it," Sadler replied. "I don't know what happens after you die and, honestly, I don't know that I want to know. Some things we're just better off not knowing."

Nax turned back to the prayer rugs. "An interesting point of view. I don't know that I agree."

"Okay, how about this," Sadler said. "Let's say you knew that Grace was going to die when she went down to Carlock, but you couldn't do anything about it. You couldn't affect the outcome. She was going to die and you just happened to know about it in advance. You couldn't talk to her about it. You couldn't stop it. You just knew it was coming."

Nax didn't respond.

"I don't know what happens when we die," Sadler said. "And personally, I think I'm better off not knowing."

Nax still didn't say anything.

She looked at him, but his face was impassive. She chewed the inside of her cheek, rocking back on her heels, waiting to hear him say something, *anything*.

When he didn't, Sadler sighed. "Look, I'm sorry. That…wasn't appropriate. I shouldn't have said that. I'm…" She waved her hands around, as if trying to reveal some secret apology that would take back everything she said. "I'm sorry."

"There's no need to apologize," Nax said, looking at her. "I concede that you raise a valid point."

Sadler's eyebrows went up in surprise. "I do?"

"I don't agree with it," he continued. "But I can certainly see its validity."

She frowned. "Oh, I'll bet you're real fun to debate with."

Before Nax could respond, the ship-wide intercom went off and Captain Mitchell said, "Will my senior staff please report to the bridge."

Sadler puffed out her cheeks in exhaustion. "There goes the rest of my night."

4

"This seems like a bad idea," Ensign Erin Calloway said.

Nobody seemed to hear her. Or if they did, they were pointedly ignoring her.

Calloway frowned and looked down at the type two fusion rifle in her hands. It felt weird. Like some kind of alien object. At the Academy, Tactical Training had been one of the few areas that she truly excelled. Out of her graduating class she had one of the highest accuracy ratings on the fusion rifle. But that was the Academy and this was a shooting range on a starship out in the middle of nowhere.

The shooting range was located on deck ten near the aft of the ship. She wasn't entirely sure, but Calloway thought one of the walls in the room was attached to an exterior bulkhead, which seemed like it made for a questionable location for a shooting range. Of course, she could be wrong. After all, she got lost three separate times on her way here.

Calloway cleared her throat loudly, but neither of the two men present bothered to glance at her.

"Seriously," the young redhead said, raising her voice. "This really feels like a *really* bad idea. Like, *really, really* bad."

The dark haired man standing across from her at the console tossed her a battery for the rifle. Calloway caught it with all the grace of a woman who was afraid she was going to blast a gaping hole in the hull of the ship and get everyone sucked out into the cold void of space.

"It's a blank charge," he said. "Just enough punch to hit the target. Other than that, it wouldn't even scratch the wall." Lt. Commander Cayden Keane was the Chief Tactical Officer on the *Defiance* and generally considered to be a handsome man. He had a crooked smile and a patchy beard. His brown eyes seemed laser-focused on everything all the time, creating an intense impression that was popular among many of the single women on the *Defiance*. Keane carried himself with confidence and walked with an unmistakable swagger. For the past few weeks, however, his swagger was a little less impressive due to the metal brace that was attached to his left leg. The cane he carried with him sat leaning against the console.

"That's great," Calloway said, looking at the square-shaped charge in her hand with an obvious lack of enthusiasm. "Now I don't have to worry about killing us all in the shooting range. Which just leaves me with the constant dread that I'm going to somehow get us all killed when I'm being counted on to keep everyone safe."

Keane turned from the console to look at her. "What?"

"Am I missing something here?" Calloway asked.

"I think that's my line," Keane replied.

"Seriously? Come on." She pointed to his left leg. "That's practically my fault."

He tapped the metal brace. "This is not your fault."

"I didn't say that it was my fault," she replied. "I said it was *practically* my fault. Which means, it could have been my fault. Or, at the very least, I contributed to it by at least ten percent."

"Ten percent?"

"At least," Calloway said. "It's basic responsibility math."

Keane just stared at her. "What the hell are you talking about?"

"Basic responsibility math," she repeated.

"I still have no idea what you're talking about."

"How do you not know what this is?" Calloway asked. "Responsibility math."

"Probably because it sounds like something stupid and crazy," Keane said. "And I save all my allotments for stupid and crazy for kinds of things that people regret the next morning. And responsibility math does not sound like that." He tapped the metal brace again. "This wasn't your fault."

"I was there on Carlock when you got injured."

"Doesn't make it your fault."

"You got injured running after me because I was some kind of space case in the middle of an engagement with a hostile entity."

Keane paused for a moment, tilting his head side to side. "Well, yes. But still, it's not your fault. I probably would have gotten nicked no matter what."

Calloway hopped off her seat and held out the fusion rifle in one hand and the blank charge in another. "Look, I am not security officer material. I *will* get somebody *killed*. That is basically a guarantee at this point."

She stood there, waiting for Keane to take the rifle and the charge.

"Okay. Right." Keane turned back to the console. "You're doing one of those crazy talk things. Alright. You do that. Based on past experience, you don't actually need me for one of those."

Calloway walked up to him. "Hello? You're not listening."

"That was the point."

"I really shouldn't be here."

"In my professional opinion, I believe otherwise," Keane said.

"I'll admit, I haven't known you very long," Calloway said. "But in the short time that I have, I get the impression that your opinions kind of suck."

He looked over his shoulder at her.

Calloway shrank back. "Please don't write me up. I thought this was a safe space."

"Safe space?"

"Well, to be fair." She held up the rifle. "I'm holding this and you're not. Which, now that I say that out loud does make it sound like I'm threatening a superior officer, which I'm totally not. Seriously, please do not write me up."

In what appeared to be one smooth motion, Keane turned around and snatched both the rifle and the battery charge from her, loading it into the rifle, clicking off the safety and leveling it at Calloway.

Calloway stared down the barrel of the rifle nervously. "Well, that was certainly impressive. Is that a requirement? Because not only can I not do that, but it's highly unlikely I will ever be able to do that."

Keane sighed and flipped the rifle over, handing it back to her. "Despite that, I still believe you should be here and the captain agrees with me."

"How? Why? Are you blackmailing the captain?"

"Okay, first off, don't go around suggesting that I'm blackmailing the captain. For that matter, don't suggest that anyone's blackmailing the captain. That's the kind of crazy talk that will definitely get you a court-martial."

"See, right there," Calloway said. "You said I'm *crazy*."

"Actually, I said 'crazy talk.'"

"Why would you want a crazy person on your security team?"

"Well, for starters, have you met Zemble?" He nodded at the large Elwat setting up targets. "Fun fact about him: He believes that when we die all the good little boys and girls get to go to Heaven and hang out with an old guy in robes and all the bad little children are going to burn for all eternity in Hell."

Zemble glared at him. "Hey!"

Keane waved him off. "I'm just trying to make a point. You believe whatever you want to believe." He turned back to Calloway. "Seriously, though, you realize that most depictions of the Devil look a lot like Zemble?"

"Come on," Zemble said. "That's not cool."

"Just trying to make a point."

"That you're an asshole?"

"I'm your superior officer."

"Who's definitely an asshole."

Keane rolled his eyes. "You understand my point?" he asked her.

"Is it that you're disturbingly insensitive towards your subordinates religious choices?" Calloway asked hesitantly.

"What? No." Keane shook his head. "Crazy is subjective."

Calloway looked at Zemble and then back at Keane. "I don't think that's how that works."

"Have you met Lt. Shadika?" Keane asked.

"No."

"She worships this clay ball that glows purple every six hours."

Zemble walked over to them. He towered over pretty much everyone on the *Defiance*. His skin was a deep dark red and there were tiny nubs that protruded from the top of his forehead. Zemble's ears jutted out slightly like fins and extended down into a neck that was as wide as his chest. "Hold on a second, you are not seriously comparing my faith in God to Shadika claiming that as long she bows before her glowing ball every day she'll never get sick?"

"I'm just making a point about how one person's crazy is another's strict religious text," Keane said.

"To be honest, I'm feeling very uncomfortable right now," Calloway said. "And I'm also very confused. And I can't decide which one I'm feeling the most strongly right now."

Keane pinched the bridge of his nose. "This is going way off track here."

"Exactly how many people on this ship do you think are crazy?" Calloway asked.

"*Everyone*," Keane replied.

"And now I'm a little afraid," Calloway said.

"It's not-" Keane cut himself off and shook his head. "Everyone's a little crazy. That's my point."

"*That* was your point? That seems like…Honestly, I don't know what that seems like. " Calloway looked at Zemble. "Are you as confused as I am?"

"No," Zemble replied. "But that's only because I've been working with him for too long."

Calloway turned back to Keane. "None of this helps me understand why you think it's a good idea for me to be here."

Keane tapped something on the console behind him. On the other end of the range six targets lit up. He grabbed Calloway by the shoulders and turned her to face the targets. "Shoot."

"What?" Calloway tensed up, fumbling with the rifle.

"Shoot," he repeated.

Calloway glanced at Zemble who just shrugged.

She held up the rifle and the six targets started moving, zooming their way around the shooting range.

"Okay, that's just not going to happen," she said.

"Shoot," Keane repeated.

"You cannot possibly expect me to hit any of those," Calloway said. "I mean, look how fast they're moving."

"Not every target is going to be polite and considerate and just stand still while you shoot at them."

"Well, Vulderran monks will," Zemble said.

Keane shot him a look.

"Never mind," Zemble muttered under his breath.

"See, that's the sort of thing that a security officer should know and I didn't know that," Calloway said.

Keane pointed at the moving targets. "Shoot."

"Seriously? Come on. This is some kind of joke, right? Like, a hazing thing? A prank for the new girl?"

"If you don't shoot now, I'm going to put a blindfold on you and then make you shoot."

"Okay, *now* I *know* this is a joke."

Keane grabbed her by the shoulders again and turned her back towards the targets. "*Shoot.* That is a direct order from your superior officer. If you don't shoot I *will* write you up."

"Okay. Fine." Calloway held the rifle up to her eye line. "No need to get nasty about it."

Then the targets sped up.

"Now they're moving faster," she said.

"Then I guess when I told you to shoot earlier you should have listened to me," Keane said. "They're just going to get faster if you don't shoot them. So do it now while it's still easy."

"Easy?" Calloway muttered under her breath, trying to focus on one specific target. "This is supposed to be *easy*? In what galaxy is this easy?" She twitched slightly and tried to recall something useful her instructor back in Tactical Training taught her.

Not a single thing came to mind.

"Screw it," she muttered and took a deep breath. On the exhale, Calloway pulled the trigger.

Six shots later, each target was registered with a direct hit and powered down.

Calloway lowered the rifle in surprise. She looked at Zemble who look even more surprised than her. She turned around to face Keane and he didn't seem surprised at all.

There was a loud squawk from the ship-wide intercom, followed by, Captain Mitchell. "Will my senior staff please report to the bridge."

Keane pushed off from the console, grabbing his cane. He nodded at the six dead targets. "*That's* why I think you belong here."

5

"MR. WARRICK-!" An explosion of sparks cut Doctor Marlize Dheer off before she could go any further. She took a step back from the open crawlspace, brushing her dark hair back behind her ear.

Dheer expected to hear some kind of yelp or exclamation of pain following the explosion of sparks, instead there was nothing but silence.

That silence was quickly broken by a raspy voice speaking what sounded like garbled nonsense. For a moment, Dheer was concerned and took a step forward back towards the crawlspace, before recognizing the language and its intent: Vulderran curses.

"Mr. Warrick?" she tried again. "Are you okay?"

The cursing immediately stopped. There was the sound of somebody attempting to move around in the crawlspace, followed by a loud *thunk* and more cursing. This time, Dheer was pretty sure he was cursing in Xensi. Which was rather remarkable for a human, considering the Xensi had no tongues and their language was structured around a series of hoots and hollers.

The individual in the crawlspace eventually switched to English as he popped out, head first. He was dressed in the same black and grey jumpsuit Dheer wore. Only where Dheer's badge over her left breast was white for Medical, his, under the oil and grime, was a dull green for Engineering.

"Westin, you Vulderran ass pimple, I hope you were looking forward to spending the rest of your career strapped to the hull of this ship, scrubbing every damn inch of it with a Fe'ihrek toothbrush."

Jaxson Warrick, the Chief Engineer for the *Defiance* gave Dheer an awkward smile that was barely visible under his bushy beard and the grime that covered the rest of his face. "Ah, Doctor." He paused, his eyes flicking around as he made sure no one else was present. "Sorry, I thought you were somebody else."

Dheer leaned in, wrinkling her nose slightly at the vague electrical smell that was wafting off of him. "Are you okay? That looked like it hurt."

"What? Oh, that little light show?" Warrick gave a dismissive laugh. "That was nothing."

Dheer frowned, not looking convinced.

"Sure, it rattled my teeth a little bit, but it's nothing that hasn't happened to me a thousand times already," Warrick said.

Dheer paused. "That sounds rather...concerning."

Warrick shrugged. "Only the first few times. After that, it feels kind of like someone's tickling you just under your skin.

Dheer's brow furrowed. "That doesn't sound any better."

"Well, I don't know what to tell you, Doc," he said. "I'd invite you to experience it yourself, but that doesn't feel like something I should be suggesting to a member of the medical field."

"I'd agree with that."

"So, is there a reason you're standing around here…?"

"You weren't answering your comm," she said.

Warrick flicked his eyes back towards the crawlspace that the rest of his short, squat body was encased in. "I'm a wee bit busy."

"So I see."

He sighed. "Look, this isn't about the power converters in sickbay, is it? I told the old bastard-"

"Please don't call Doctor Rabkin that," she interrupted.

"What? He's old."

"No one is disputing that."

"And he's most definitely a bastard."

Dheer didn't defend the point, but she didn't argue it either.

"It's not like I haven't already called him that to his face."

"So I've noticed," she replied dryly.

"Look," Warrick said with a tired sigh. "Like I told Rabkin, I'll have Westin look into it as soon as she's done reprograming the secondary food processors."

"Before or after you send her out to the hull with the Fe'ihrek toothbrush?"

"Before," Warrick replied with a straight face.

Dheer just nodded.

"I understand, medical is really supposed to take priority," Warrick said. "But if those food processors go out again, we're going to end up with a lot of crewmen with low blood sugar around here. I can't speak for your department, but my boys in Engineering get cranky when their blood sugar gets low. So, if you don't mind, Doc, I really need to get back to work here."

Before Warrick could wiggle his way back into the crawlspace, Dheer cleared her throat loudly and folded her arms.

"Actually, Mr. Warrick, while I appreciate the repair update, I'm actually here about *you*."

Warrick stopped wiggling around and raised both eyebrows. "I beg your pardon, ma'am?"

"I've been going over the crew medical reports and I've noticed something rather disturbing."

"We all have way too much iron in our systems? That's not my fault. I've told the Capt'n a thousand times we need a new ventilation system around here. You know how much crap we're all breathing in on a regular basis? I can change the filters every damn day, but it doesn't change the fact that the system is barely catching thirty percent of the garbage in the air."

Dheer pressed her lips together tightly. "No, but thank you for bringing *that* to my attention."

"Then what the hell are you bothering me for?" Warrick asked. "No offense, but I'm in the middle of replacing the thermal particle matrix here."

"Mr. Warrick, do you realize it's been two years since you've been in for a physical?"

"So?"

"Every crew member is required to submit to an annual physical," Dheer said.

Warrick didn't say anything. Somewhere in the crawl-space something clanked and rattled. Something green and yellow leaked out of the crawlspace, dripping down just past Warrick's head. It slowly puddled its way towards Dheer.

"I wouldn't let that touch me if I were you," Warrick warned her.

Dheer stepped left of Warrick and the puddle, which now had a vague glow about it. "Will it hurt me?"

"Nah," Warrick said. "It's just Qeebvavan oil. It'll just leave you smelling like a Fim'ai ass fart for days." He paused and then added, "Well, weeks, really. The only way to get the smell out is with a static particle bath and that, of course, will basically leave every inch of your body stinging for another few days."

Dheer wrinkled her nose and took another step away from the glowing puddle. "So noted."

"Doctor," Warrick said. "Have you heard the rumors about how the only things keeping this ship from falling apart are basically my bare hands?"

"Yes."

"They're rumors based in a lot of truth. I don't have a lot of time to spend sitting around getting looked over by you or the old bastard. When I'm not feeling well or West-in's poked me with her damn plasma torch again, I'll come by and get patched up. Beyond that, my schedule's booked solid. So, if you'll excuse me…"

"Actually, no I won't," Dheer said.

"Sorry now?"

"Not only were you not answering your comm-"

"It's basically impossible for me to reach it while I'm here," Warrick said, kicking his foot against the crawlspace.

"-but you've been avoiding or straight up ignoring every message I've sent you for the last two weeks about this," Dheer finished.

"When I said that I was holding this ship together with my bare hands, I wasn't speaking in metaphors," Warrick replied. "Last week I literally held the bulkhead on deck twelve together for almost forty minutes before we were able to get a sealant in place on the outside."

Dheer squatted down next to his upside down head. "In addition-"

"Nothing good ever follows those two words," Warrick grumbled.

"In addition," Dheer repeated, "I also discovered that we don't have any medical history on file for you from before you joined the *Defiance*."

Warrick opened his mouth and then closed it. Neither of them spoke for a moment.

"I've got nothing clever to say," Warrick admitted finally.

"I'm not looking for anything clever, Mr. Warrick," Dheer said. "I'm just looking for your information."

Warrick shifted uncomfortably in the entrance of the crawlspace. "If it helps at all, I've never really been great at making medical appointments."

"As I'm sure you can imagine, that doesn't help."

He sighed. "Look, Doc, I've been…around."

"So I've heard."

"Before I joined up with the Fleet, the longest I spent in any one place was on Natuzzi and they didn't exactly have any doctors there that were familiar with basic human anatomy," he said. "It's not like I've had the opportunity to get a family doctor, if you know what I mean."

"As I understand it, you and Mr. Nax spent some time as Vulderran monks."

Warrick rolled his eyes. "Yeah, sure. That's the one everybody loves to bring up. Nobody ever mentions the months we spent in the Iddad system helping the Xensi science police stop idiots from surfing across that damn black hole."

Dheer raised an eyebrow. "I was not aware of that particular story."

"See. There's more to my past than a few misguided years hanging around a Vulderran temple."

"*Years*, Mr. Warrick?"

Warrick gritted his teeth. "It was *complicated*."

"I'm sure it was." She paused and then said, "As I recall, somebody mentioned something about it involving a woman?"

Warrick's shoulder jerked like he wanted to point at her. "If you were a *man*, you'd find yourself in some really complicated situations too if it involved an *Urliean woman*."

"You know that one out of every six men that engage in sexual intercourse with an Urliean female end up dead, right?"

"Well, sure," Warrick replied with a smile. "It's part of the *allure*."

Dheer rubbed a hand over her face. "Mr. Warrick…"

"I told you it was complicated," he said.

She took a deep breath and exhaled slowly. "I understand that you spent some time on Taupeer Prime?"

"Yeah, sure. Nax and I ended up down there when we ran out of credits and got kicked off our transport vessel. We spent four months working on the repair crew for their remote miners until we had enough saved up to get off planet."

"Most Taupeerens carry a small viral infection that remains dormant their entire lives. However, it can be passed along to non-Taupeerens, usually through saliva and most commonly through sexual intercourse. In humans, this infection can riddle the brain with tiny lesions that result in micro-strokes that are practically undetectable."

"I was inoculated for that," Warrick replied.

"And some of those inoculations have been known to

create complications even years later when combined with something as simple as a flu shot," Dheer said.

Warrick squinted at her. "Really? Nobody told me that."

Dheer sighed again. "Mr. Warrick, it's not healthy for you to live like this."

"I would strongly disagree with that, considering that I'm here today to have this pointless conversation with you."

She held up one finger. "It only takes one instance for something to go horribly wrong and then you end up dead because your doctor didn't know that you had an allergy to some basic neuro-stimulant."

"It also only takes one ion coil to overheat and wipe out the entire engineering department," Warrick replied.

"Which is why you make sure to routinely check up on the ion engines and ensure they're well maintained so that the coils don't overheat," Dheer said.

"Son of a bitch," Warrick muttered.

"I'm assuming that means I've made my point?" Dheer asked. "I don't have to continue with my analogy? I can, if you'd like. Your body, this ship-"

He shook his head. "I know when I'm beat."

"So I can expect to you see in my office tomorrow?"

Warrick made a face. "Sure."

The ship-wide intercom squawked and Captain Mitchell said, "Will my senior staff please report to the bridge."

Another Vulderran curse escaped Warrick. "So much for getting anything productive done."

6

"Did you hear that Zemble started up a damn bible study?" Doctor James Rabkin asked.

Rabkin was the oldest man on the *Defiance* and he looked every bit of it. He had a full head of bold white hair that was long overdue for a trim. His face looked like weathered granite that was about a thousand years old and finally showing its age. But his hands remained as steady as they had been in his twenties and his brain was twice as sharp.

On the other side of the black quartz chessboard Captain Gavin Mitchell stroked his chin as his green eyes flicked up from the board momentarily. "That's not how I would have put it."

Mitchell was still several decades younger than his old friend, and he was handling his approaching fifties with grace. He had a strong square jaw and his hair was mostly grey at this point, save for a few handful of dark streaks that were determined to stick around for as long as possible.

"That's because you don't have the same way with words that I do," Rabkin said.

Mitchell turned his attention back to the board. "But, yes. I heard about it."

"And?"

Mitchell glanced up at his old friend again. "And I also heard that you attended it."

"You say that like it's a bad thing," Rabkin replied with a grumpy frown. "Personally, I figure it's best to stay on good terms with a higher power. You never know when you'll need an act of God to intervene in the surgical bay."

The two men sat at the table in Mitchell's quarters. The chessboard between them was still fairly undisturbed, despite the fact the two men had been at the game for a little over an hour now.

"Is there a point to this, old man, or are you just gearing up for another soapbox rant?" Mitchell asked.

Rabkin sat back in his seat, folding his arms. "What point? Why's everything got to be a damn rant?"

"I've been trying to ask you for the last twenty years," Mitchell replied. "You always seem to dodge the question."

"I'm just trying to make conversation."

"Case in point."

"Doing my best to make my constant aging as comfortable as possible."

"What the hell are you going on about, old man?" Mitchell asked.

Rabkin pointed at the chessboard. "I'm trying to find a graceful way to point out that you haven't made a damn move in over fifteen minutes and I ain't getting any younger."

Mitchell looked up at him again. "You have somewhere to be?"

"It's not so much that I have somewhere to be, as it is

that I don't want this game to be my dying act all because you wanted to figure out how to beat me in ten moves."

Mitchell sat back from the board without making a move and grabbed his drink, taking a slow sip.

Rabkin glared at him. "Now you're just being an asshole."

"It's called strategic planning," he said.

"You can call it whatever you want. You're still being an asshole."

"Sure," Mitchell agreed, setting his glass down. "But I'll be the asshole who had you beat three moves into the game."

Rabkin leaned forward, propping his forearms on his legs. "You know what your problem is?"

"I'm too damn competitive."

Rabkin just gave him a grumpy glare and got to his feet with a loud groan. He walked over to the liquor cabinet Mitchell kept. After a minute or so of rummaging around the bottles, he said, "Your other problem is that you have shit taste in alcohol."

"Have I ever told you how much I've appreciated your friendship over the decades?" Mitchell asked.

"No and I'm pretty sure that if you did say it, you'd be spewing a line of bullshit."

"Because I won't let you retire."

Rabkin grabbed a bottle of Backlon brandy and made his way back to the table with another nasty glare. "Stop that."

Mitchell finally picked up his pawn and moved it two spaces.

"That's it? Almost twenty minutes and that's the best you could come up with?" Rabkin poured himself two fingers of the blue colored swill.

"Old man, the game's already over," Mitchell said, finishing off his drink. "I've got you beat in eleven moves."

"Eleven?" Rabkin studied the board for a moment as he sipped his drink. "You losing your edge in your old age?"

"Just thought I'd give you an extra opportunity to beat me this time."

"Oh? Wow. A whole extra move. Your generosity astounds me." Rabkin moved his bishop, taking Mitchell's pawn. "Has it ever occurred to you that I've been letting you win all these years?"

"Once or twice," Mitchell admitted. "But then I remember how much of an old bastard you are and old bastards don't ever let anybody else win just because."

"Maybe," Rabkin agreed. "But then, maybe I'm playing the long con. I could be setting you up for an epic takedown any day now."

Mitchell looked at him, unimpressed. "Twenty years is a hell of a long con."

"Patience is a virtue."

"Not one of yours, old man." Mitchell moved another pawn.

Rabkin took another sip from his drink. "You're an asshole." He moved his rook and sat back down. "You should visit it."

"What?"

"Zemble's bible study," Rabkin said. "It behooves a captain to know what his people believe in."

"'My brethren, be not many masters, knowing that we shall receive the greater condemnation.'" Mitchell replied.

"Am I supposed to be impressed that you can quote scripture?"

"Let's just say that I don't think it would be a great idea

if I were to start dropping in on my crew's off-duty activities," Mitchell said.

"Uh-huh."

"If you've got something to say, old man, just say it. It's not like you to make me push for it."

Rabkin rolled his empty glass back and forth between his hands, not saying anything for a moment. He studied the board.

Mitchell looked at him, an impatient expression on his face.

"Heard some news about your ex-wife the other day," Rabkin said finally.

"Which one?" Mitchell asked.

"Well, considering I don't count the second one, I must be talking about Johanna."

Mitchell sighed loudly. "Just because you didn't like Keiko-"

"Nobody liked her," Rabkin cut him off. "Nobody liked her because she was a damn Dishan and nobody in their right mind likes *mind readers*. Including *you*."

"I *married* her," Mitchell pointed out.

"And I warned you not to," Rabkin said, pointing an accusatory finger at him. "You can't hide a damn thing from those mind reading bastards. I told you it was going to come back and bite you in the ass. And what happened? It came back and bit you in the ass."

Mitchell rubbed his forehead tiredly. "How many times have you been married again?"

"Three more than you and not once to a damn mind reader." Rabkin tapped his temple. "The kind of shit that goes on in here is liable to get me killed if I was married to a mind reader."

"I can't imagine it's any worse than what comes out of your mouth," Mitchell said.

"At least I go to my grave knowing that my dirty thoughts about my second-in-command didn't get me thrown into the damn doghouse."

Mitchell looked at him coolly. "Do I have to remind you that I'm still the captain?"

"Trust me, you don't have to remind me," Rabkin said. "I remind myself every time I draft a new resignation letter for you to ignore."

"I don't ignore them," Mitchell replied. "I read every single one. I just don't approve them. What did you hear about Johanna?"

Rabkin grunted and took a deep breath, exhaling slowly. "Ambassador Dupree recently relocated to Starbase Sixty-Four. Where she's heading up a new diplomatic team to re-engage potential peace talks with the Phaw."

Mitchell didn't say anything. He just stared at the board, his hands folded beneath his mouth.

"I bring this up because, despite the fact that the two of you separated a decade ago, it wouldn't be such a bad idea for you to pass along some form of congratulations," Rabkin added.

Mitchell still didn't say anything.

Rabkin grabbed the bottle of Backlon brandy and poured himself two more fingers. "Of course, you could just ignore me and blow the whole thing off. It's not like she was the best thing that literally ever happened to you."

Mitchell finally looked up at him. "Old man, are you trying to play matchmaker?"

Rabkin shrugged. "Starbase Sixty-Four is only a week and a half trip from the *Atlantic*. This is the closest the two of you have been in seven years. Could be there's a higher power trying to tell you something."

Mitchell turned back to the board and moved his

queen. "Or it could be you're just trying to play mind games with me. Checkmate."

Rabkin spat out his drink. "What the hell happened to eleven moves?"

"Part of the overall strategy," Mitchell said, getting to his feet.

"Where you straight up lie to me?"

"I won didn't I?"

Rabkin frowned. "You already knew about Johanna, didn't you?"

"Yes."

"How?"

"I know how to read a news item."

"You are an asshole." Rabkin shook his head. "You've got a damn alert set up, don't you? Goes off any time there's an item about her in the news."

Mitchell didn't respond. He walked over to the window and watched the passing stars.

Rabkin got back to his feet with another groan. "You know, Starbase Sixty-Four is still pretty close. I'm sure one of us could work out an excuse for the *Defiance* to make a trip out there."

When Mitchell still didn't say anything, Rabkin took the hint and changed the subject.

"Heard an interesting rumor about your new first officer." Rabkin picked up the black knight and looked it over. There was a deep scratch along its back. It was old and mostly smoothed over and now it looked like a gentle groove.

Mitchell grunted, not bothering to look away from the window. "Broderick Cooper."

Rabkin looked up from the marble piece in his hand. "So you've heard the same rumor then?"

"I read the report that was issued to me," Mitchell said.

"Straight from the horse's mouth?"

"Pretty much."

"Any truth to the rumors?"

"Depends on what you heard."

Rabkin set the knight back on the board. "Heard he's an asshole that likes kissing other assholes."

Mitchell looked back at Rabkin with a raised eyebrow.

"Obviously I'm paraphrasing," Rabkin added.

"Obviously."

"McNeely back on the *Atlantic* worked with him on the *Orion*," Rabkin said. "Said he's the kind of guy who'll suck up to whoever he has to in order to get a promotion and if that doesn't work, Cooper's been known to stab a few officers in the back to get ahead."

"Allegedly," Mitchell added for him.

Rabkin grunted. "Sure. *Allegedly*."

"What else did you hear?" Mitchell said.

Rabkin rubbed the palm of his left hand over his right knuckles. "Well, Mora Tsuang out at the base on Tarterous Prime said he's a big fan of the Burning Phoenixes team on Castor Six. So regardless of anything else, this Broderick Cooper clearly has very low standards and is probably the scum of the galaxy."

Mitchell rolled his eyes and shook his head. "The Phoenixes are a fine team."

"Sure they are." Rabkin nodded. "If you're a blind, deaf mute who needs something to cheer for in their life."

"None of that's in his record," Mitchell said.

"I'm not surprised," Rabkin said. "Just another example of the higher-ups trying to sweep the uncomfortable darkness we've all got to live with under the rug."

"He's on track for his own command in probably less than a year," Mitchell said. "He's not going to be with us very long."

"Just long enough to stab you in the back."

Mitchell turned away from the window, but didn't say anything.

"We both know Sadler should be taking that spot," Rabkin said.

"I could offer her the position gift wrapped with a sizable sign-on bonus and she'd still turn it down," Mitchell said.

"Then she'd be a fool."

"Besides, Wanamaker made it clear it was out of our hands," Mitchell said. "Cooper's placement comes straight from the office of the President."

"Because a politician is exactly the sort of person you want finding you a first officer for an assignment out here in the middle of nowhere, next door to a hostile empire that's looking to start a fight."

"Based on his record Cooper sounds like he'll be a fine first officer."

"For you or President D'Ambra?" Rabkin asked.

"What's the status with Calloway?" Mitchell asked, changing the subject.

Rabkin sighed and shook his head again. "Nothing new. All of her vitals remain stable and she hasn't exhibited anything remotely similar to what she did back on Carlock."

"Any other tests we can run?"

"Not before she starts getting suspicious," Rabkin said. "I'm running out of excuses to take weekly blood samples as it is. Also, Dheer is having…issues."

Mitchell looked back at him. "With what?"

"Not telling Calloway what happened back on Carlock."

Now it was Mitchell's turn to shake his head.

"And, honestly, I don't think she's wrong," Rabkin

added. "At some point we're going to have to admit that we're at a dead end and sometimes the only way through a dead end is by smashing through it."

Before Mitchell could respond, there was a soft chime and the computer announced, "Incoming encrypted transmission from Starbase *Atlantic*."

Mitchell walked over to his desk. "Mitchell Alpha Riptide Eight."

The floating graphic of the UPA logo disappeared from the console screen and Kathryn Straub appeared in a pre-recorded message.

"Gavin, sorry for the recording, but I don't have time to chitchat. One of our sensor buoys in the Uslen system just picked up an S.O.S signal. I'm ordering the *Defiance* to intercept, investigate and provide any potential assistance that may be needed."

"The Uslen system?" Rabkin said. "We're at least four hours from there. There's got to be somebody closer."

Mitchell wordlessly turned the console screen around so that Rabkin could see the video playback from the sensor buoy.

"Well, ain't that a son of a bitch," Rabkin muttered as he watched the wormhole open.

Mitchell opened a channel on the ship-wide intercom. "Will my senior staff please report to the bridge."

7

"THIS IS Captain Gavin Mitchell of the *USS Defiance* to the unidentified vessel in distress, do you read us?"

There was no response.

On the viewscreen the unidentified vessel sat floating in the emptiness of space, tilted at a slight angle compared to the *Defiance*. It was easily four times the size of the *Defiance* with a long fuselage that was capped off on one end with a wide saucer section and a twin set of engines on the other side that looked like they hadn't been used in years.

Mitchell swiveled in his command chair to face Calloway at the comm station. "Anything?"

She shook her head. "Sorry, Captain."

"What about that Morse code transmission?" he asked.

Calloway double checked her console. "It's being transmitted from the vessel."

"I suppose it would be weird if we tried to just call them using Morse code ourselves, right?" Rabkin asked from beside Mitchell.

"Put it on the speakers," Mitchell said, turning back to the viewscreen.

The Morse code transmission played out over the bridge speakers. A series of audible dots and dashes that to everyone on the bridge sounded like nothing more than empty static.

"Damn creepy is what that is," Rabkin said.

Mitchell exhaled. "You ain't lying." He scratched his cheek and gestured for Calloway to turn it off. "Mr. Keane, tell me something useful."

From the tactical station, Keane scanned his console as he made an uncomfortable face, "Like they said at the *Atlantic*. The first few seconds are a standard S.O.S. After that, it's basically gibberish. Computer can't make heads or tails of it and neither can anyone else."

"That's the opposite of what he asked for," Rabkin said.

Mitchell looked at him. "Are you confused?"

"About what?"

"Your role on this ship," Mitchell said. "You're the doctor, not my mouthpiece."

Rabkin's bushy eyebrows furrowed. "No reason I can't be both."

Mitchell turned to Keane. "It can't just be gibberish."

Keane shook his head. "A handful of random words, numbers and equations that don't add up to anything. That's the textbook definition of gibberish, Captain."

"Morse code." Mitchell drummed his fingers against the armrest of his command chair. "When was the last time anybody used that?"

"According to the computer, over four hundred years ago," Keane said.

"Hell of a place for it to show up again," Mitchell said. He glanced at Rabkin. "Any insights, old man?"

"What the hell are you asking me for?" Rabkin grumbled. "I'm a doctor, not a damn codebreaker."

"True," Mitchell agreed. "But you are the only one around here old enough to remember when Morse code was last used."

"You're hilarious," Rabkin replied flatly.

Mitchell clapped his hands together loudly. "Somebody's got to have something useful for me. I can't make an informed command decision if I don't get any information."

"Hasn't stopped you yet," Rabkin said.

"You know, the only thing stopping me from ordering Keane to have you escorted off the bridge is the fact that I'm afraid he's going to break you in the process," Mitchell said.

"I don't know. Sounds like a pretty nice paid vacation for me," Rabkin said with a smile.

"Captain, I may have something," Sadler said.

"It better be something good, Commander."

On the viewscreen, several sections of the vessel were highlighted.

Sadler gestured to the highlighted areas. "Sensors picked these up. They look like scorch marks from a possible attack."

Mitchell leaned forward. "Okay, now we're getting somewhere."

"Sensors can't seem to identify any familiar energy patterns, though," Sadler continued.

"That's what happens when you start counting your chickens before the eggs hatch," Rabkin chimed in.

Mitchell ignored him. "Life signs?"

Sadler shook her head. "Nothing that our sensors are picking up."

"There has to be *somebody* over there," Calloway said. "I mean, who set off the distress signal?"

"Sure somebody sent the transmission," Rabkin said.

"That doesn't mean they're still alive. After all, sweetheart, it is a distress signal."

"Oh," Calloway whispered. "Right."

"Vessel looks to be running on maybe reserve power?" Sadler said, studying her console. "We're not picking up any major energy sources on the ship. The engines look like they haven't been powered up in a while. In fact," she paused, double checking something. "If the sensors are right, that vessel out there is easily four or five hundred years old. Maybe even older."

Rabkin gave a low whistle. "Well, there's something you don't hear every day. When was the last time you heard about a ship that old still being used?"

"The Cucae," Mitchell replied. "But, hell, they're nomads. They don't build their ships to last, their whole civilization is going to fall apart."

"Still," Rabkin said. "I don't think I've ever heard of a Cucae ship that was older than maybe one fifty." He nodded at the vessel on the viewscreen. "And that's a hell of a lot bigger than anything the Cucae built."

Mitchell just nodded.

"Half the vessel seems uninhabitable," Sadler said. "Possibly due to any potential damage from whatever attacked them. But the areas that do have power are showing a human friendly atmosphere. A very friendly human atmosphere, in fact."

Mitchell stroked his chin, glancing over at his second-in-command. "A boarding party?"

Sadler shrugged. "Could be the only way we find out what's going on."

"No way in hell I'm going over there," Calloway said from her console. "Especially not if they're all already dead."

Mitchell and Rabkin turn to look at her.

Calloway's face quickly matched her red hair. "Oh, boy. I said that out loud, didn't I? I didn't mean to say that out loud. Not that it sounds any better if it's just in my head. I mean, thinking it is really just as bad as saying it, right? At least, that's what my mom always taught me: Thoughts can be just as bad as actions. Which sounds kind of stupid now that I'm saying it out loud." She shrunk back in her seat. "Please don't kick me off the ship," she whispered.

Mitchell smiled and turned back to the viewscreen. "No worries, Ms. Calloway."

"That's good," Rabkin said, nodding his head. "Plausible deniability."

"For what?" Calloway asked hesitantly.

"In case you end up on the wrong side of an airlock," Rabkin said.

Mitchell shot the old man a look. "Stop it."

"What?" Rabkin shrugged. "I'm just doing my part."

"And what part is that?"

Rabkin shrugged again. "I feel like it changes from day to day. But today it's keeping the newbies on their toes."

"Ms. Calloway?" Mitchell said.

"Yes, sir?"

"Feel free to ignore the doctor."

"Yes, sir," she replied, not really sounding any more relieved.

"Hey, now you're undermining my authority as the medical professional around here," Rabkin complained.

"Feel free to ignore the doctor on anything that isn't medical related," Mitchell amended. "Now, before I authorize an away team to go board the mysterious vessel out in the middle of nowhere, can anybody even tell me where it came from? There's supposed to be a wormhole around here?"

"If it's anything like the one we ran into back in the Neutral Zone, we're not going to know its there until we're right on top of it," Keane said.

"Any idea where it's supposed to be?" Mitchell asked.

"Based on the data from the sensor buoy and the ship's current trajectory, somewhere in this vicinity," Nax replied, highlighting a section on the screen that was approximately forty parsecs away from the unidentified vessel.

"And where is that sensor buoy?" Mitchell asked. "*Atlantic* said it stopped transmitting shortly after our friend showed up."

Nobody answered.

Mitchell spun around in his command chair. "Seriously? Anybody?"

"It's not popping up on any of our sensors," Sadler said.

"Is that irony?" Rabkin asked. "Our sensors can't find our sensor buoy? That sounds like irony to me."

Mitchell leaned forward, rubbing his hands together as he studied the vessel on the viewscreen. "Mr. Keane?"

"Sir?"

"You've been keeping tabs on the decoding of all the data we pulled from the Veneer base on Carlock, right?"

"Yes, sir."

"What did they know about the wormhole?"

"Well, they were certainly using it," Keane said. "Beyond that, doesn't look like they knew much else about it."

"Have we been able to link it to the Unity?" Mitchell asked.

Keane took a deep breath before answering. "Technically, no. But, my gut says that it's no coincidence that there was an active, stable wormhole in the vicinity of where there was a known Unity incursion."

"What about the Veneer? Anything in the data that suggests they knew about a connection?"

Keane shook his head. "All the data is from the Veneer point of view. Communication between them and the Unity was extremely limited. If it was something that came up, it wasn't recorded anywhere. But honestly, I don't think it was an issue that was a priority for the Veneer on Carlock."

"What's on your mind, Gavin?" Rabkin asked quietly.

"A lot of things," Mitchell replied. "None of them are going to help me sleep at night if any of them are true." He got to his feet. "Who else is out here?"

"Well, the Uslen system is basically uninhabited. Vurit is about ten lightyears out," Sadler replied from her console. "After that, there's the Inni and then the Neutral Zone. Nearest shipping route is over eight lightyears away from here."

"Mr. Nax," Mitchell said. "Do you think you could get a shuttle over there?"

"I believe I have located an accessible docking port," he replied. "Based on these readings it should be compatible with our systems."

"That's damn convenient," Rabkin said.

"They're putting out a Morse code transmission, old man," Mitchell said. "It isn't surprising either. Mr. Keane, who else uses Morse code?"

"Based on my research, both the Tegis and the Yumu'll use something similar," Keane replied. "But humans are the only ones to use anything that would have been identified by our systems as Morse code."

Mitchell looked at Rabkin expectantly.

"You mean to tell me you think that's one of ours out there?" Rabkin asked, pointing to the vessel.

"Simplest answer," Mitchell replied.

"Sure, let's go with that," Rabkin said sarcastically. "Never mind it doesn't look like anything we've built *ever*. And let's also ignore the fact that we're not exactly known for building ships that last as long as that one has. Let's ignore all that."

"Okay, sure," Mitchell agreed. "It all seems like pretty relevant data, but I'll play Devil's Advocate with you."

Rabkin glared at him. "What the hell is a human vessel doing popping out of a damn wormhole we didn't know anything about before a month ago?"

"Just because it's the simplest answer doesn't mean it's the easiest one," Mitchell said.

"The hell kind of answer is *that*?"

"Best you're going to get, old man." Mitchell turned to Nax. "Mr. Nax, how do you feel about taking a field trip?"

"I would love the opportunity to stretch my legs."

"Good. Put together a team and get over there and get me some answers."

"Captain," Sadler started to say.

"You think that's a wise idea?" Rabkin asked, beating her to it.

Mitchell looked at Sadler and Rabkin before asking Nax, "Commander, is there something I should be aware of?"

Nax got to his feet, clasping his hands behind his back. "I believe the doctor and the commander are concerned about my current state of wellbeing in regards to me leading an away mission."

Mitchell waved a hand around. "Which means, what exactly?"

"It means he hasn't slept in five weeks," Rabkin said.

Both of Mitchell's eyebrows went up. "Is this true?"

Nax nodded. "I'm afraid so, Captain. I seem to be afflicted with a slight case of insomnia."

"A slight case of insomnia is when you're occasionally up half the night," Rabkin said. "What you have is a bizarre medical phenomenon that's never been documented before."

"Doctor, as I recall, there is supposed to be something regarding doctor/patient confidentiality," Nax said.

"Sure," Rabkin said. "But I get to wave that any time I feel like my patient is about to make a stupid decision." He turned to Mitchell. "Don't take this the wrong way, but you've got to be out of your damn mind if you let him head up that away team."

"What other way is there to take that?" Mitchell asked dryly.

"The man hasn't slept in five weeks," Rabkin said.

"Doctor," Nax said. "If you don't mind me asking, how many Natuzzi have you had the opportunity to examine before me?"

Rabkin frowned, his brow furrowing in frustration as he immediately saw where this was going. "None. Because you crazy bastards refuse to leave your damn planet."

Nax nodded, calmly ignoring the jab. "So you don't have any previous medical experience by which to compare my current status against?"

"Look, common sense is the same whether you're born on Earth, Natuzzi or the galaxy's asshole, Phaw Prime," Rabkin said.

"Then I would argue that you are hardly in a place to position yourself as an expert on Natuzzi physiology," Nax said.

Rabkin took a step forward, waving his finger at Nax. "Now wait just a damn minute-"

Mitchell held up a hand, cutting the doctor off. "I'm not interested in watching two of my senior officers get into a shouting match on my bridge."

"It is not my intention to start a fight, Captain," Nax said. "I am just attempting to address the concerns the doctor has."

"You've got a funny way of doing it," Rabkin grumbled.

"This isn't my ideal setting for this conversation either," Nax replied coolly. "Captain, I don't believe anyone has registered a complaint regarding my service during the last five weeks, have they?"

Mitchell glanced at Sadler who shook her head. "No, I don't believe so."

Again, Nax nodded. "Then, Captain, I would submit that my current sleeping difficulties have failed to negatively impact my abilities to serve on board this ship in any capacity."

Mitchell didn't say anything for a moment. "Mr. Nax, I understand that you've been having some difficulty regarding the death of Commander Hawkins."

"Not in any way that would affect my abilities to serve, Captain," Nax replied.

Mitchell tilted his head to the side. "Can you offer an explanation for your current lack of sleep?"

"I'm afraid I cannot," Nax admitted. "However, I can assure you that it hasn't negatively impacted me."

"Tell me something, Mr. Nax, are you a doctor?" Rabkin asked.

"No."

"Any experience in the medical field?" Rabkin asked.

"No."

Rabkin nodded. "So where the hell do you get off

saying that your lack of sleep hasn't negatively affected you?"

Mitchell turned to Rabkin. "Okay, you need to dial it back a little bit."

"Until you accept any one of my letters of resignation, I'm still the Chief Medical Officer on this damn ship," Rabkin said.

Mitchell sighed and pinched the bridge of his nose. "Look, do you have anything on file that would suggest that Mr. Nax is not capable of doing his job?"

"You mean other than the fact he hasn't slept in the last five weeks?" Rabkin asked.

"Which is something you've failed to bring up until now," Mitchell pointed out.

Rabkin folded his arms. "It's a little thing called doctor/patient confidentiality."

Mitchell just shook his head and turned back to his helmsman. "Mr. Nax, if you think your current condition won't compromise the away team in any way, then by all means, take the field trip."

Rabkin's nostrils flared. "Are you out of your damn-"

"Do me a favor, old man," Mitchell said, cutting him off. "Wait till we're in private before you try to chew me out."

Keane cleared his throat, getting to his feet. "If you don't mind, Captain, I'd like to tag along."

Mitchell pointed over his shoulder towards the lift. "Go ahead, Commander."

Keane grabbed his cane and followed Nax.

"That sounds like a great idea," Rabkin said. "You've got a severe insomniac whose judgment may be impaired and a cripple. We got anybody around here who's blind that we can send along?"

"I don't know about blind," Mitchell said. "But I've

certainly got a grumpy old ass man who I can send over there.

Rabkin folded his arms. "No way in hell I'm going over there."

Mitchell shook his head and glanced back at Calloway. "And you wonder where the kids get it from."

8

"BLOODY HELL," Warrick whispered, staring out the front window of the shuttle. "If I wasn't seeing it with my own two eyes, I wouldn't believe it."

Ahead of them the mysterious vessel loomed even larger than it had on the *Defiance's* viewscreens. The shuttle's tracking lights flashed across its surface, revealing it to be more stone-like in its appearance. Within the small confines of the shuttle, the vessel seemed to stretch out for miles.

Nax piloted the shuttle in a gentle, almost gliding approach towards the vessel, taking the scenic route to the docking port he had spotted earlier.

Warrick leaned forward in his seat, trying to get a closer look. "There is no possible way this thing is space worthy."

"And yet," Dheer said from her seat behind Nax, "here it is in space."

Warrick shook his head. "No, just because it's out here doesn't mean it belongs out here. This design doesn't make any damn sense. Look at those lines." He gestured at what appeared to be ragged seams along the ship's surface. "The damn thing looks like it's been carved right out of a mountain. This looks like somebody strapped a couple of engines on the back of an asteroid and decided to call it a ship."

"Could be collected space debris," Keane said. "If it's as old as the sensors are scanning it to be."

Warrick stroked his beard. "I don't know. I've heard rumors of ships like that. Generational ships. Built to last thousands of years, transporting an entire civilization from one end of the galaxy to the other."

"And?" Keane said.

"I thought it was a load of Iarctec eel shit back then and I still think it is now," Warrick replied.

"Mr. Warrick, has anyone ever told you that you have a very specific way with words?" Dheer asked.

Warrick glanced back at her and smiled. "Thank you."

"Wasn't intended as a compliment," she said.

"Jaxson subscribes to a very specific theory of space travel," Nax explained, taking the shuttle under the fuselage of the vessel.

"I subscribe to the same theory of space travel as everyone else," Warrick said. "It's called the common sense theory. You don't build something that's too damn big."

"That doesn't seem like much of a theory," Dheer said.

"Exactly," Warrick said. "It doesn't need to be much of a theory because that's how reality works. Any time I hear someone going on about building these massive ships designed to last for five hundred years or more, I ask them why? What's the point of building something to last that long when it's going to be outdated in half the time?"

Nax brought them out from under the fuselage and alongside it.

"You want to go traveling around the galaxy in a ship

the Fleet built two hundred years ago?" Warrick continued. "I sure as hell don't. You think the *Defiance* is
cramped? Back then, they were basically building oversized
tin boxes with rockets on them. You want to rely on the
most advanced technology from two hundred years ago?
Because that's what you're asking for with a ship like that.
No, thank you."

"So you think the sensors are off?" Keane asked.

"I *know* the sensors are off," Warrick said. "I've told the
captain a hundred times that the entire sensor array needs
to be completely redone. We're working with equipment
that's not only outdated, but it's also being held together by
Qeebvavan tape and about thirty yards of Vulderran electrical tape. So, yeah, the sensors are off. But they're not off
enough to misread the quantum dating on this thing. My
people aren't that sloppy."

"So what?" Keane asked.

"Hell if I know," Warrick said. "There's only so much
you can tell from the outside of a ship." He looked at Nax.
"You know what it reminds me of?"

"The shipwrecks on Luma Four," Nax said.

"The shipwrecks on Luma Four," Warrick agreed. He
pointed to the section of the fuselage that appeared to be
twisting out as though it was a natural extension. "Look at
that. What the hell is that even supposed to be? It's just like
the Ka'anphoi spires."

"Indeed," Nax agreed.

"Wait a minute," Keane said, getting up from his seat.
He limped his way up to the front of the shuttle, holding
on to the wall for support.

Dheer frowned, glancing at the metal brace on Keane's
leg. "You shouldn't be out here," she said quietly.

"And pass up this opportunity?" Keane shook his head.
He pointed at the ship. "You see that? That right there is

why I signed up with the Fleet. Strange, mysterious star-ships that no one's ever seen before?

"Of course," Dheer said dryly. "I don't know what I was thinking. Who could possibly resist this tantalizing mystery in space."

"You joke," Keane said. "But if my fourteen-year-old self could see me now he'd be freaking out."

Warrick held up a fist. "Preach it, brother."

Keane fist bumped the chief engineer. "Amen."

Dheer pulled out her scanner and waved it over his leg.

"Stop it," Keane said, trying to move away from her.

"You're lucky we didn't have to replace the entire leg," she said.

"So you've mentioned already," Keane replied. "Honestly, having a bionic leg replacement would fit my brand better at this point."

Dheer rolled her eyes.

"Although," Keane continued, "I can't decide which would play better on sympathy from the fairer sex. It might take too long to explain that my leg is fake, versus a beautiful lady just spotting the brace right away."

Dheer put her scanner away. "Cayden, you suffered a serious injury and if I had my way, you'd be on desk duty back at the *Atlantic* for the next six months. You're still very vulnerable to potential infections and who knows what we could find over there."

He held up his hand. "I'll be extra careful not to get myself nicked."

"It's not that simple," she said.

"I'll be fine," Keane said. "*We'll* be fine." He nodded at the ship. "Whoever or whatever was on that ship is long dead."

"Let's hope that whatever killed them isn't still there, then," Dheer said.

"If the occupants of this vessel passed away from old age, then I'm afraid that their killer will most definitely still be present," Nax said.

"What the hell is that supposed to mean?" Keane asked.

"Time," Warrick said. "He's talking about time. It's his idea of a joke."

Nax smirked.

Keane just shook his head. He turned back to Warrick. "Were you talking about the shipwreck graveyard on Luma Four?"

"Yep," Warrick replied. "Now there's a thing of haunting beauty that you'll be dreaming about 'till your dying days."

"It's impressive," Nax said. "But I doubt you'll be haunted by it."

"Don't listen to this orange bastard," Warrick said. "He thinks every sunrise is a work of art. But a graveyard filled with ancient, behemoth ships that have been just sitting there for thousands of years? He shrugs it off like its a damn Fim'ai child's finger painting. To anyone else who lays eyes on it, its the kind of thing that haunts your dreams."

"And how the hell did you get to see it?" Keane asked, the jealousy in his voice barely contained. "The entire Luma system is off limits to the Alliance."

Warrick and Nax exchanged a brief look.

"It's…a long story," Nax said finally.

"One best told over Kusalax ale," Warrick said. "So you remember as few of the potentially incriminating details as possible."

"Nobody knows how the ships of the Luma Graveyard ended up there," Nax said. "The Luma government has historical records documenting their existence as far back as almost eight hundred years ago, although there are records that suggest several of the ships there are much older than that."

"That's what's supposed to happen to ships over a certain age," Warrick said. "They either get blasted into space dust or they end up in a graveyard on some desolate planet nobody's allowed to visit. They don't float around the galaxy, popping out of wormholes." He gestured at the scorch marks along the fuselage. "Those are definitely from some kind of attack. Looks like it might be from a particle cannon. Maybe even a plasma array?"

"That'd be either a Phaw ship or even an Oxean Syndicate vessel," Keane said. "But we're too far for either of them."

"We don't know where the other end of that wormhole opens out to," Warrick pointed out. He squinted at something along the side of the fuselage. "What the hell is *that*?"

Nax adjusted the shuttle's spotlight so it was pointed in the direction Warrick was looking at.

Keane shook his head. "I can't make it out."

Warrick unbuckled himself from his seat and moved to the rear window to get a better look at the markings on the ship. "Looks like letters of some kind. Maybe the ship's name?" He moved back to his console and redirected the shuttle's sensors for a closer look.

A moment later, on a side screen, an image appeared of the markings.

"Look familiar to anybody?" Warrick asked.

Nax shook his head. "I'm afraid it's not a language I'm familiar with."

"Me neither," Keane said.

Warrick tilted his head, as if he was trying to see what it looked like upside down. "Kind of looks like Sweezakaal, but there aren't enough inkblots for it."

"I know what it is," Dheer said. "It's not used very often anymore. Only a handful of provinces still speak it, but it's essentially a dead language back home."

Keane looked at her. "Home?"

"Earth." Dheer nodded at the markings on the screen. "It's Chinese. Whatever this is, it's definitely from Earth."

9

"*THE ETERNAL HAND OF GOD*," Sadler announced from her console. "That's what it translates to."

"And I thought the *Defiance* was pretentious," Rabkin said.

On the viewscreen there was an enhanced version of the markings the shuttle had found. Under the image Sadler's translation quickly appeared.

Mitchell looked at his chief medical officer. "What the hell is pretentious about *Defiance*?"

"Sounds like we're going around looking for a damn fight."

"How is that pretentious?"

"Because we behave like we're not flying around in a bucket of bolts that are held together with Qeebvavan tape and string," Rabkin said.

"String?"

Rabkin shrugged. "The hell should I know what Warrick's doing? All I know is I was visiting Ensign Brynne in his quarters on deck four and the damn door was held in place with rope."

"I'm not having this conversation anymore." Mitchell turned to Sadler. "*The Eternal Hand of God?*"

"Catchy name isn't it?" She looked up from her console. "According to the computer there's never been a single ship in the history of the Fleet to go by that designation."

"You had to check the computer for that?" Rabkin asked. "I'm pretty sure we'd all remember if we had a ship that went by *The Eternal Hand of God*. I don't care how long ago it was."

"Also," Sadler continued, "Chinese isn't exactly a language that's been popular for the last couple of centuries. In fact, it meets all the requirements for a dead language."

"There are requirements for that now?" Rabkin asked.

"I don't know how on top of your history any of you are," Sadler said. "But the Chinese basically ceased being a culture of any prominence in the early part of the Twenty-First century after it was hit with a super virus that reduced the population by over eighty percent."

"Chairman Mao's Superflu," Rabkin said. "Read about that one in medical school."

"You sure you didn't learn about it first hand?" Mitchell asked.

"Popular theory was that it was designed by the Chinese government itself as a form of a population control." Rabkin shook his head, a distant look in his eyes. "That's some real scary shit there."

"As popular a theory as it was, it was never proven," Sadler said.

"Probably because the virus took out all the people who could prove it," Rabkin said.

"Regardless of where it came from, after it made its way through mainland China, there wasn't much left,"

Sadler said. "It swept through in about six months. The existing infrastructure couldn't handle the abrupt loss of life and that was it. The Chinese government was essentially shut down. Russia and India came in to help and ended up divvying up the land and what was left of their resources. The language continued to be used for the next fifty years or so. But eventually, it faded away as the surviving generation died off. And that was basically the end of the Chinese culture."

"And before that?" Mitchell asked.

"Before that, China had a deep history of huge manufacturing plants," Sadler said. "But they were building things for other people. They didn't have much of a space program. All the first faster-than-light engines were built post the China collapse. There's no way they built that." She nodded at the ship on the screen.

"So where the hell did it come from?" Mitchell asked.

Sadler just shrugged. "I have no idea, Captain."

"Secret space program?" Rabkin suggested. "They had a secret population control program."

Sadler shook her head. "Based on the historical records, there is no conceivable way that ship was built on or near Earth."

"Sure," Rabkin said. "But historical records are so reliable and history is never recorded by people with an agenda."

"You're more conspiracy focused than usual," Mitchell said. "You forget to take one of your pills?"

"Just checking to make sure you were still paying attention to me," Rabkin said. "If I'm gonna be stuck around here, I want to make sure I'm not talking to myself."

"What are the odds there's another alien race out there that has a language structure similar to China's?" Mitchell asked.

"Highly unlikely," Sadler replied. "This isn't like Morse code. The Chinese language is too complicated, too specific, for it to be confused with something else. And besides," she gestured to the translation on the screen. "It was an exact translation. The computer didn't even pause."

Mitchell sat back in his chair, rubbing his hand over his chin. "This doesn't make sense."

"Sure it does," Rabkin said. "In fact, it makes about as much sense as ignoring your chief medical officer and letting your sleep deprived helmsman head up the away mission to look into the mystery ship."

Mitchell shot him a sideways look. "You got something you want to say, old man?"

"Nothing you haven't already ignored," Rabkin replied.

"Maybe you should file a complaint," Mitchell suggested.

"Is it going to get me off this ship?"

"Probably not."

"I'm pretty sure I've got better ways to waste my time, then."

Sadler made a weird noise under her breath that caught Mitchell's attention. She quickly turned her attention back to her console.

"Okay." Mitchell got to his feet. "Both of you. My office, now."

10

———————

AFTER THE CAPTAIN disappeared into his office with Rabkin and Sadler, Zemble felt a weird sensation at his back, like somebody was staring at him. He twisted in his seat at the tactical station and found Calloway looking at him.

"What?" he asked.

"What?" Calloway asked back.

Zemble frowned. "You're staring."

Calloway blinked and looked nervously around the bridge, as though she hadn't been aware of how long she had been staring. "Oh, uh, I, um, sorry." She turned back to her own console and focused aimlessly on the screens for a moment. She looked back up at Zemble, who was still waiting patiently. "I have a question."

"I figured."

"And it's kind of an, um," she rolled her lips together, "inappropriate question, I think? Maybe?"

Zemble's horns bunched together as his brow furrowed. "What is it?"

Calloway held up a hand, her fingers twitching around. "Well, it's about your…religion, I guess."

"My religion?"

"Your faith? Is that a better way to put it?"

"Is that your question?"

She shook her head. "Well, it's just, uh, you're, um, a Christian, right? That's what it's called?"

Zemble stared at her for a moment and then said, "That's your question?"

"Well, it's just…" she trailed off for a moment, looking around the bridge like there was somebody she could rope in for support. Finally she looked back at Zemble. "I just don't know how to ask this without sounding like some backwater hick who didn't even leave her own planet until after her twenty-third birthday."

Zemble sat up straight and folded his arms. "Okay, this should be interesting."

Calloway cleared her throat. "It's just that, well, I know that, technically, Christianity isn't a human-centric religion. But it is kind of human-centric, isn't it?" She tilted her head to the side.

"Is God human-centric?" Zemble asked.

"Well, I mean…" Calloway scratched her nose. "We, humans, were supposedly created in His image. So, you know…" She shrugged.

"And what part of building a personal relationship with God is considered human-centric?" Zemble asked.

"Yeah, but, like I went to church every Sunday morning growing up and, like, is our God your God? I mean, can our God be your God? Like, don't you have to have your own God or something." Calloway held up both hands. "Okay, this is making me sound way more xenophobic than I am. Because I'm not. Xenophobic, that is. I get along with everybody. I mean, I haven't met a lot of aliens, true. You're, like, the fourth or fifth alien I've met? But everybody's great. You especially." She made a face and a hand went to her mouth. "I'm not hitting on you. I swear. And that's not because I'm not into non-humans. Because I'm sure that, you know, in totally different circumstances, I would *totally* be into you. You're great and now it sounds like I'm hitting on you again and I can't seem to stop."

Zemble held up a hand to silence her. "It's fine."

Calloway bit her lip. "Is it? Because it doesn't feel particularly fine." She waved a hand at her face. "Are you warm? Because I'm feeling very warm."

"You're also almost as red as I am."

Calloway's head bobbed up and down. "Right. Right. Um, who do I have to get permission from in order to leave the bridge so that I can go find a quiet corner and die?"

"It's fine," Zemble said. "I understand what you're getting at."

"You do? Because even I don't know what I'm saying anymore."

"It's really not that complicated," he said. "The message of the Bible-"

Calloway smacked her face. "I didn't even think about the *Bible*. How does that even *translate*?"

"For starters, it's shorter."

"Shorter?"

"We didn't cut anything out," Zemble said. "We just use less words. What takes you ten words to describe in Earth Standard, we do it in five."

Calloway paused. "Is this like a competitive thing?"

"No," he said. "It's a 'your language is very ineffective' thing."

"I'm pretty sure that's more xenophobic than anything I've said so far."

"Look, God is *God*," Zemble said. "That's the whole

point of God. If He can create one form of life, He can create multiple."

"Well, sure, but…"

"Look, what you really want to know is how I ended up a Christian."

Calloway nodded hesitantly. "Yes, I think so."

Zemble shifted in his seat and his back cracked. "About a generation or so before Elwat joined the UPA the Evangelical Church of Christ sent a crew of missionaries to our home planet. I remember reading that was one of the largest missionary assignments in the history of the church. The Word of God really connected with my people and took off pretty fast. By the time we joined the Alliance, over half our population identified as Christians," Zemble explained. "It's the largest organized religion on my planet."

"That's kind of crazy," Calloway said.

Zemble shrugged. "How much do you know about Elwat?"

"Apparently not enough not to sound like a xenophobic racist."

He waved her off. "You're fine."

"Am I?"

"I mean, you're not calling me crazy," Zemble said. "So you're already a step ahead of Keane."

Calloway tilted her head to the side. "Okay. Fair point."

"He's not that bad, really," Zemble said. "I think one of these days I'm gonna get through to him."

"You're gonna, what, convert him?"

He nodded. "Yeah, I've made it a personal mission of mine. Before I transfer to another ship, I'm gonna get him turned around."

"I'm going to be honest with you, this is so *weird*," she whispered.

"Well, before the church came along, we were all worshiping a dead tree."

"And it gets *weirder*."

"And you thought Lieutenant Shadika's clay ball sounded weird, right?"

"A dead tree?"

He shook his head. "That is too complicated to explain. Point is, my people were lost and hungry, spiritually speaking, and when the church arrived, we devoured it."

"Wow," she breathed. "I still have so many questions."

"Like?"

"The Bible doesn't say anything about anyone other than humans," she said, nodding her head. "That's a big one."

"Did you think that God personally handcrafted life on Earth and left the rest of the cosmos to figure it out on their own?" Zemble asked.

"Well, no, I don't think so," Calloway said. "I mean, I kind of didn't really think about it at all..."

"They don't talk about it in the Fleet Academy," Zemble said, "but there's actually a Christ-like story on almost half the planets in the UPA."

Calloway looked at him dubiously. "Seriously?"

He nodded. "The Old Testament details are never quite the same. But the story of Creation and God sending his only Son as the ultimate sacrifice? Practically universal concepts. Even on the Backlon home world."

Calloway folded her arms. "Okay, now I know you're screwing with me."

Zemble shook his head and held up his right hand.

"Hand to God, I swear. The natives on Akmar Four, one of the most famous pleasure planets in the galaxy, have a Christ story that dates back a solid two thousand years before they even ventured into space." He gestured at her console. "You can see for yourself. Sure, it's not something they go around advertising next to their banner ads for their brothels, but it's there. Lieutenant Shadika? She worships that glowing ball of hers, but a third of her planet believes in the story of Eesa M'aseeh, which is remarkably similar to the story of Jesus. They even have a lot of the same iconography."

Calloway didn't say anything. She just squinted him suspiciously.

Zemble shrugged. "Sin is a universal concept and so is God. You should come to my Bible study. We go over a lot of this."

"There's *more*?"

"It's a big galaxy."

"It's a weird galaxy."

"You have no idea," he said. "On Viha Six He's even called *Jesus*. There's no translation into their language. It's just Jesus."

"You can't possibly expect me to believe that."

He pointed to her console again. "Look it up for yourself."

"This is by far, the weirdest conversation I have ever had," Calloway said.

Zemble chuckled and turned back to his console. "Wait till you talk to an Ovvin about their mating rituals."

11

"OKAY, which one of you wants to tell me what the hell is going on?" Mitchell asked, sitting down behind his desk in the small office that was adjacent to the bridge.

Sadler and Rabkin looked at each other, but didn't say anything.

Mitchell held out his hands expectantly. "Well?"

Rabkin took the seat across from Mitchell. "What do you want me to say? You already let him lead the damn away team. It's a little late to advise you on anything."

Mitchell glared at him and then turned to Sadler. "Commander?"

Sadler clasped her hands behind her back so she could fidget with her fingers without either the captain or the doctor noticing. "I'm not entirely certain I should say anything."

Mitchell folded his hands on the desk. "Commander, I understand that you're not angling for a promotion here. In fact, you've actively avoided any promotion for the last four years. But here's the thing, with Commander Hawkins gone, you're my number two."

"Captain, I don't feel comfortable-"

"I don't give a damn whether or not you feel comfortable," Mitchell cut her off. "The job description doesn't say anything about getting to be comfortable."

Rabkin nodded. "Amen to that."

"Old man, you're not out of the fire yourself," Mitchell said.

"Hey, if you don't like the way I do my business, feel free to kick me off the ship," Rabkin said. "I've got my eye on a sweet retirement pad on Akmar Four. It's right across the street from one of the most exclusive nudist beaches in the Alliance."

Mitchell turned back to Sadler. "This is what happens when you spend your entire career trying to buck responsibility."

"Don't listen to him," Rabkin said. "I was plenty responsible when I was your age. Hell, I made Chief Medical Officer on the *Blackwell* six months before I turned thirty. I was the youngest CMO for almost two decades before that diaper wearing savant came around and got promoted to CMO at nineteen." He shook his head.

"Damnit, Jim," Mitchell said.

"What the hell do you want me to tell you, Gavin?"

"I want you to tell me if there's something wrong with one of my crew," Mitchell snapped. "I shouldn't be learning about these things five seconds after I've sent one of them off to lead a potentially dangerous away mission."

"The thing is, Gavin, Nax isn't wrong," Rabkin said. "I don't know enough about Natuzzi physiology to say if there's anything wrong with him. For all I know, most Natuzzi men go through some kind of sleep deprivation around his age. Who knows? It's not like I can get any data from the Natuzzi government and Nax himself isn't exactly the most helpful when it comes to Natuzzi biology."

"But he came to you about his sleep disorder?"

"Yeah," Rabkin said. "After about a week of no sleep he stopped by sickbay and asked me to look him over." The old man shrugged. "But what was I looking for? I have no damn idea. I ask Nax, and he just gives me some vague bullshit. You know how he can talk in circles without ever saying anything. I prescribed him a new exercise routine and a new diet. I told him if he was still having problems in a week come back. He did. I gave him some homeopathic stuff to help with his natural sleep rhythms and gave him the same spiel. Week later, he's back and still not sleeping. I put in a request to the Natuzzi government for some basic Natuzzi male benchmarks and they told me to go fly a damn kite."

Mitchell gave him a tired look. "Really?"

"I'm paraphrasing, obviously," Rabkin said. "Like I said, I don't know what to tell you and that's why I didn't tell you anything. Obviously, whatever it is, it isn't affecting him. At least not in any way that I can determine. Nobody's complained about him. He hasn't been overly emotional. He hasn't shown up late for his duty shifts. He doesn't seem to be showing any lapses in judgment. He hasn't seemed to have forgotten anything from his skillsets. Hell, for all I know, he's going through some kind of late-onset Natuzzi puberty."

"Natuzzi…puberty?"

"What part of 'I have no damn idea' do you not get?"

"It's not that," Sadler finally spoke up.

Rabkin and Mitchell turned to her.

"Then what is it, Commander?" Mitchell asked.

She paused before answering.

"I don't want to have to give you some kind of speech," Mitchell said.

"And you don't want him to do it," Rabkin added. "He's terrible at it."

Sadler exhaled slowly. "It's about Hawkins."

Rabkin's bushy eyebrows went up and leaned back in his chair. "Well, that was going to be my next guess."

Sadler looked Mitchell in the eye. "Sir, I want you to know that I feel really uncomfortable talking about this."

"You're going to have to get over it," he said. "It's part of the job."

"I don't really want the job."

Mitchell shrugged. "Sometimes we don't get what we want."

"I know that I sure as hell don't," Rabkin muttered.

Mitchell nodded at her with his chin. "What's going on?"

Sadler moved her hands in front of her, pressing them together as if she was about to pray. "Well, as we all know, Nax and Commander Hawkins were in a...relationship."

"Half the ship knew," Rabkin said. "They weren't exactly being subtle about it. They couldn't keep their damn hands off each other." He looked at Mitchell. "Did I tell you one of my nurses caught the two of them in the medical storage unit on deck four?"

"Let's not speak ill of the dead, old man," Mitchell said.

"I haven't gotten to the ill part," Rabkin said. "When I start talking about how they were humping like rabbits in heat every damn day, then you'll know I'm at the ill part."

"Jim..."

"Besides," Rabkin said, "it's not like Nax is dead."

"I don't think it was simply a physical relationship," Sadler said.

"You an expert in interpersonal relationships, Commander?" Rabkin asked.

"Actually," Sadler said, "I minored in psychology at the Academy."

Rabkin squirmed in his seat. "Well then, maybe you can help me figure out why I have a bad habit of sticking my foot in my mouth."

"That would be a waste of time," Mitchell said. "So Commander Hawkins and Nax were, what?"

"In love, I believe," Sadler replied. "Although, based on what little conversation I've had with Nax, I'm not certain he's even aware of it."

Rabkin folded his arms. "Yep. You definitely took some psychology classes."

"On top of that, as it's been explained to me, Nax doesn't have any form of reference for how to grieve," Sadler said.

"What the hell does that mean?" Mitchell asked.

"Oh, *this* I've heard about," Rabkin said, sitting forward again. "The Natuzzi's belief system is centered around universal harmony or some such hogwash. Anything that's dead or destroyed, isn't really dead or destroyed, it's just been repurposed towards achieving universal harmony."

"Okay, that seems fairly harmless," Mitchell said.

"Except that it's been explained to me that anyone who's not Natuzzi doesn't really count towards this universal harmony," Sadler said.

Rabkin shook a finger at her. "That part I haven't heard about."

Mitchell leaned forward, resting his forearms on his desk. "What exactly does that mean, Sadie?"

Sadler gesticulated with her hands for a moment, as if trying to pluck some kind of explanation from the air. "I'll be honest, Captain, I'm not entirely certain. But I think it basically comes down to the fact that the rest of us don't count."

Mitchell raised an eyebrow. "We don't *count*?"

She shrugged. "It's how it was explained to me."

"Sure casts a lot of their behavior in a different light," Rabkin said. "Instead of them just keeping to themselves because they're a bunch of xenophobic assholes, it's actually because they're a bunch of xenophobic snobs."

"Where exactly did you get this information?" Mitchell asked.

Sadler didn't answer right away. The expression on her face was conflicted.

Rabkin gave her an encouraging wave. "In for a penny, in for a pound."

Sadler sighed. "Warrick help shed some light on the matter."

"Of course it was Warrick," Rabkin said. "Who the hell else is it going to be?"

"I'm more interested in why he didn't bring it to my attention," Mitchell said.

"It's not like he went out of the way to tell me," Sadler said. "I kind of asked about it."

"Which then makes me ask why haven't *you* brought it to my attention?" Mitchell asked.

Sadler swallowed nervously. "I didn't really think it was my place to say anything, Captain. I mean, honestly, I only found out about his sleeping disorder today. Before that, it was just the wailing."

"I'm sorry, Commander, did you just say *wailing*?" Mitchell asked.

"Apparently it's an ancient Natuzzi grieving ritual," Sadler explained quietly.

Mitchell just raised an eyebrow.

"Very ancient," she added.

Mitchell took a deep breath and stretched back from his desk. "So what's the bottom line here?"

Sadler shrugged. "I don't know. I mean, as everybody's already pointed out, he seems to be doing just fine."

"Except for the fact that he's not sleeping," Mitchell said.

"And let's not forget the wailing," Rabkin reminded him.

Mitchell made a noise in the back of his throat. "What's it supposed to look like when a Natuzzi grieves?"

Nobody had an answer to that.

Mitchell took a deep breath and exhaled slowly. "Okay, how about this one: what can we do to help him? It may not be affecting him now, but eventually, Nax is going to break."

"Or he won't," Rabkin said.

"Suddenly you're Mr. Optimistic?" Mitchell asked.

Rabkin held his hands out, palms up. "When all else fails, try optimism."

"I don't think that's how that goes."

"It should."

There was a soft chime and then Calloway's voice came over the speakers, "Captain?"

Mitchell tapped a section of his desk. "Go ahead."

"Um, you might want to come back to the bridge," Calloway said hesitantly. "We have an...intruder, I think?"

Rabkin looked at Mitchell. "What the hell is that supposed to mean?"

"We either have an intruder or we don't, Ensign," Mitchell said, stepping back out onto the bridge.

Calloway just made a weird face from her console and looked at his command chair.

The command chair swiveled around. It was occupied by a man Mitchell had never meet before.

"Ah, Captain, you're done. Good. I didn't want to interrupt your meeting. That sort of thing makes a poor first impression, don't you think?"

"Who the hell are you?" Mitchell snapped.

The man paused for a moment, as if giving the question some serious consideration. "Well, why don't we just call me God."

12

———

THE FIRST THING Warrick noticed after the airlock door opened was the *silence*.

On every ship, and especially with the *Defiance*, there was some kind of background noise. The low thrum of the engines. A slight rattle in the deck plates. Muted conversation between passing crewmen. The soft whooshing of the ventilation system. They were comforting distractions from the reality that on the other side of the hull was nothing but the cold empty vacuum of space.

But here on the *Eternal Hand of God*, Jaxson Warrick heard *nothing*.

It gave him a moment's pause.

"What is it?" Nax asked his friend at the open airlock door.

"Too damn quiet," Warrick replied, clicking on his flashlight and waving it around in the darkness that was waiting for them.

Nax took a moment, listening carefully. "I don't believe I've heard such silence before on a starship."

"Sure you have," Warrick said. "The Aztix cruiser in orbit around Va'hli."

Nax raised a hairless eyebrow. "Everyone was dead on that ship, Jaxson."

Warrick just shrugged and stepped through the open airlock.

Keane and one of his security officers, Lieutenant Grell, a short, squat man with a flat nose and crooked eyes, pushed past everyone to the front. Their fusion pistols weren't drawn, but their hands rested comfortably on the leather grips. The beams of their flashlights moved in careful patterns across the open space, revealing little in the darkness.

Keane and Grell disappeared deeper into the dark. A moment later there was a grunt followed by a loud sound of metal being pushed across metal as the two men opened the next door out into the main corridor.

Dheer followed behind Nax along with Lieutenant Askon. Like all Knoks Askon had a lanky form with dark purple skin and two short antennae extending from beneath his jet black hair. He inhaled and exhaled in short, shallow breaths that seemed to echo loudly in the silence of the dead ship.

Dheer glanced back at Askon. "Are you okay, Lieutenant?"

He gave her a weak smile and his antennae twitched. "Fine." Askon's voice had a ring to it that most people could only describe as 'angelic.' "Not a fan of the darkness." His antennae twitched again. "My home planet tends to be in a state of perpetual light. Darkness is not only something we aren't accustomed to, but we have some fairly strong religious feelings towards it."

"I don't think you have anything to worry about, Lieutenant," Dheer said. "If there were any monsters on this ship, our sensors would have picked them up."

Askon gave her another weak smile. "Yes, well, the Kinqoix, which are the ancient devils my people believe exist only in darkness, have a tendency not to be detected until the last minute. Or, least, that's what all the religious texts would have you believe."

"You're supposed to be a man of science," she reminded him.

"Of course," Askon agreed. "But even scientists have been known to read a scary book or two during their impressionable youth."

Other than the silence, the darkness was the most obvious problem. Each member of the away team carried a flashlight, but despite their combined effort, it made little difference in the darkness that seemed to cover every inch of the ship.

Warrick paused for a moment, closing his eyes as he counted to ten. He clicked his light off just before he reopened his eyes.

"Commander?" Askon asked. The angelic ring in his voice did little to hide the nervousness.

"Hang on," Warrick replied, making sure he was facing away from the other members of the away team when he opened his eyes.

It took a second for his pupils to adjust, but when they did he noticed the dim, almost imperceptible lighting along the bottom edge of the walls.

Warrick knelt down to get a closer look, waving his hand under the faint blue glow.

"There's no way this ship is even running on emergency power," Warrick said. He rapped his knuckles on the paneling. "She's in some kind of sleep mode. Like a ship in space dock. No need for anything but basic life support systems."

"Light isn't considered basic life support?" Askon asked.

"Not if nobody's planning on being on board," Warrick said. "And I don't think anyone's been on board this old girl for a good long while." He wiped two fingers across the wall panel, carving out two deep trails in the thick dust. "Feels weird."

Askon stepped over and ran his scanner across the wall. "It's some kind of nadion/tellurium composite."

"Never felt anything like it before," Warrick said, brushing it off his fingers. The dust fell to the ground in thick clumps that crumbled away to nothingness. "Felt like a soft rock. Almost moist."

Askon waved his light across the wall. "It looks like the same material covering the exterior of the ship. Possibly a side effect of prolonged exposure in the wormhole?"

Warrick shook his head. "When we popped through one of those our higgs energizers ended up looking like a pair of deep-fried Draeddur turkey legs. There's no way we would have lasted any longer than we did."

"This ship was clearly built to last," Askon pointed out.

Warrick looked at him out of the corner of his eye. "You trying to say something about the *Defiance*?"

Askon's antennae turned in opposite directions. "Nothing you haven't already said."

Warrick sighed. "Ain't that the truth."

"Jaxson," Nax said. "I believe I have something over here."

Warrick got back to his feet, flicking his light back on as he looked for his friend.

Nax was on the other side of the room in front of what appeared to be a console of some kind.

Keane and Grell stepped back into the docking room from the hallway.

"Just as dark and quiet out there," Keane said. "I'm not really looking forward to stumbling around in the dark."

"What would your fourteen-year-old self say now?" Dheer asked, pulling out her scanner.

"Find a damn light switch," Keane replied. "fourteen-year-old me was terrified of the dark."

"Fourteen-year-old you?" Dheer asked dubiously.

Keane flashed his light towards her. "When I was nine I spent a year on Faecha Three. Sunset takes about three months and night lasts for another six. I don't want to say it's a scarring experience, but I had nightmares about it well into my late teens."

"I've heard that the sunsets on Faecha Three are supposed to be breathtaking," Dheer said.

"Sure," Keane said. "Breathtaking. That's exactly how a nine-year-old boy would describe it when the endless shadows start playing tricks on him, making it look like there was a damn Scuvid land shark lurking around every corner."

"I'd stop there, Doc," Grell said, smirking. "You start poking around in the Commander's subconscious and you'll never make it back."

Keane looked Grell. "You want to get transferred to the *Atlantic* and get stuck with cargo security for the next six months?"

Grell's expression turned straight. "No, sir."

"Then shut up."

Dheer suppressed a smile and nodded at the main corridor. "Any signs of life?"

"Out there?" Keane pointed back to the hallway with his thumb. "Not unless it's invisible and silent."

Warrick tapped on the console Nax had found, but

nothing lit up. He set his flashlight on its dark surface and ran his hands along the edges, looking for any seams. He found one on the front of the console, down near the floor.

Warrick grabbed a flathead spanner from his workbag and slipped the edge into the seam. It didn't take much of an effort and the panel popped right off in a small cloud of space dust.

The chief engineer coughed, waving a hand in front of his face. "Nax, point your light down here."

When Nax complied, Warrick got a good look at what appeared to be a handful of plastic bags connected to a series of circuit boards by a thick collection of barely luminescent wires.

Warrick leaned in for a closer look. "What the hell is this?"

"It would appear to be some kind of gel-powered network," Nax said.

Warrick grabbed one of the plastic bags and carefully disconnected it from the wires. "Like on Mineer, you think?"

"Possibly," Nax agreed, taking a quick count of the number of empty gel bags inside the console. "However, this seems to be a rather inefficient use of it."

"Yeah, I was thinking the same thing. On Mineer they were able to power whole houses off a single gel pack. How many are in here?"

"Fifteen," Nax replied.

"Overkill?" Warrick tore open the bag and took a sniff. Whatever it was, his face twisted up like he was smelling a dead and decaying Qeebvavan corpse.

"Perhaps a storage unit?" Nax theorized. "Auxiliary power cells for shuttles? Given our present location, it wouldn't be a stretch to imagine there's a nearby shuttle bay."

"Smell this." Warrick handed him the bag.

Nax frowned and held up a hand, gently pushing the bag away. "I'd rather not, thank you very much."

"Spoilsport," Warrick grumbled.

Keane limped over to the two men. "What does any of that mean?"

Warrick shrugged, grabbing some of the wires from the other empty gel packs. "Who knows? On Mineer, they use gel packs to power pretty much everything. However, the contents of their packs are naturally occurring fuel on their planet. It's kind of like the old fossil fuels they used to use back on Earth, except these last for months before needing to be replaced. Officially, the Alliance isn't really keen on the notion of harvesting naturally occurring fuels. But, the Mineer don't really use them off planet so the UPA tends to leave them alone. More or less." He stripped a handful of the wires, exposing copper coils underneath. "The problem is, they're more effective than our borodium batteries. You won't hear anybody officially say that. But, you get a couple of the higher ups in the Engineering Corps liquored up after hours and they'll tell you that the Mineer's gel packs have an electrical current consistency that's almost fifty percent higher than our borodium batteries."

Warrick separated the exposed wires and then reached into his workbag. After rummaging around for a second, he pulled out a datapad. He pressed his thumbs against the back casing until he heard a click and then slid it off, exposing the circuitry inside.

"I have no idea what any of that means," Keane said, slightly impatient.

"It means," Warrick replied, taking the exposed wires and connecting them to the motherboard on his datapad, "that the gel packs produce a higher voltage than the borodium batteries. It takes four borodium batteries to run the ventilation system. The Mineer could do it with two gel packs and it would probably last twice as long." He looked up at Keane. "But nobody's going to file an official report on that."

"Because if you do that," Keane finished for him. "You end with the UPA endorsing fossil fuels."

"And nobody wants to think about going around harvesting whole planets to power our ships." With the wires attached, Warrick flipped the datapad over and powered it up. "Point is, the Mineer have been careful to keep their energy tech in-house. To see something similar out here and on a ship this size?" He shook his head. "I don't know what to think of it."

The datapad flickered on for a moment and then went black again.

Warrick turned it back over and twisted one of the wires.

Immediately the datapad lit up.

In the darkness of the room, the glow of the datapad's screen was like a small sun.

Warrick blinked as his eyes adjusted to the brightness. "Since the ship is in some kind of low power mode, I'm going to try to patch into the data systems from here. Maybe find us something useful instead of stumbling around in the dark."

Keane straightened up, wincing a little as he took some of the pressure off his left leg.

"How are you doing?" Dheer asked quietly, coming up alongside.

"I'm fine, *Mom*," Keane replied.

"You know that if something goes wrong, you'll probably be the first to die," Dheer said.

"That's my job."

"It may be your job to jump in front of the laser blast," Dheer said. "But you're going to end up dead because while the rest of us are running, you're hobbling behind us."

He looked at her out of the corner of his eye. "You've been working too closely with Rabkin. Your bedside manner has gotten increasingly more…rough."

"Rough?"

"And naggy," he added.

"I'll keep that in mind the next time you come in for some painkillers," she said.

He rolled his eyes. "Our biggest threat on this ghost ship is tripping over somebody's hundred-year-old skeleton in the dark."

Dheer nodded at Askon. "The Lieutenant was telling me all about the popular nightmare myth on his planet about Kinqoix devils and how they dwell in absolute darkness."

"Seriously," he replied. "You really need to do something about your bedside manner."

After a minute of navigating through various subroutines, Warrick said, "Okay, I think I've got us a map." He held up the datapad so the rest of the away team could see what appeared to be some kind of detailed blueprint of the *Eternal Hand of God*.

He pointed to the blacked out sections at the front of the system. "Near as I can tell, they suffered some kind of hull breach in the forward part of the ship. Based on what we saw coming in, it couldn't have been anything too big. But my guess is too much of that part of the ship depressurized before they could get any seals in place.

"It looks like our initial sensor readings were accurate," he continued. "There's no one else on this ship. You can see here where the ship's systems are acknowledging us."

He pointed at six yellow dots on the screen. "If there was anyone else onboard, they're long dead."

"There you go," Keane said to Dheer. "Now you can stop worrying and just focus on whether or not I'm going to trip in the dark."

Warrick gestured towards the rear of the ship. "This looks like engineering. At least, it's where I'd put engineering, based on what looks like the fuel feed lines and their connection to the main engines. If we could get down there, I might be able to restore main power. Or at least enough power to get the lights turned back on and maybe pull up the main systems. However," Warrick used two fingers to swipe up and magnify a section of the ship near the top. "This is the interesting part. According to this, this section here? It has *full* power."

"How's that?" Keane asked.

Warrick shrugged. "Could be any number of things. The section could be running off its own independent power supply. Could be a subroutine programmed into the main system that keeps it up and running while the rest of the ship is powered down. Could just be an error in the ship's internal sensors. Like I said, this old bird is just running enough juice to keep basic life support up. After that? The computer doesn't really care about anything else."

Keane looked at Nax. "Engineering could get us main power back."

"And with main power restored, it would certainly make it easier to investigate this vessel," Nax agreed.

"But that section that's already powered up..." Keane trailed off.

Nax nodded. "It does pose a rather interesting question."

Keane grinned. "That's not exactly how I would put it.

But if you're suggesting we should give it a look-see, I totally agree."

"Of course you would," Dheer said.

"How big is this section?" Nax asked Warrick.

Warrick scratched the back of his bald head, studying the screen. "Hard to say. A lot of these measurements don't make any sense." He looked up at Nax. "The size of the main cargo deck back on the *Defiance*? Little bigger maybe? It's also where the distress signal is originating from. Which makes sense, given it's the only place with enough power to transmit anything on this space heap."

"Which is going to be easier to get to?" Nax asked.

"Oh, it's going to be like navigating the Murpilax Desert Death Trail to get to either of them," Warrick said. "With the main power out, we're going to be stumbling in the dark. Both this powered up section and engineering are at least three or more decks above us. Which means climbing, since none of the lifts are probably going to be powered up. Although this," he pointed to what looked like a path on the blueprint, "could be some kind of ramp or ascending tunnel? It was probably meant for something else, but with the main power down, we could probably walk through without any problems and that could shave off quite a bit of climbing up to that powered section."

Nax didn't say anything for a moment. He silently studied the blueprint on Warrick's datapad, weighing the various options available to him.

And then, for the briefest of moments, Nax saw Grace Hawkins' reflection in Warrick's datapad.

It startled him.

He glanced back over his shoulder in the direction she should have been in order for her reflection to appear on the datapad, but, of course, there was no one there.

Nax turned back to Warrick and the datapad, but there was nothing but the blueprint present on it.

"Something wrong?" Warrick asked.

Nax shook his head. "In the interest of time, I believe we should split into two teams." He paused again, almost imperceptibly so this time, as if waiting to see if her reflection would appear again.

It didn't.

Looking at the rest of the away team, Nax continued, "Given Mr. Keane's current condition, I suggest that he, Mr. Askon and Doctor Dheer investigate the powered section of the ship. Jaxson, Grell and I will make our way to engineering and get main power restored." He paused and then added, "Does anyone have any concerns they would care to share?"

"Yes, but I don't think anyone's going to listen," Dheer said, glancing at Keane.

Warrick got to his feet. "I'll transfer the map to everyone's pad."

"Let's proceed with caution," Nax said. "Although, I find it doubtful that, given the current condition of the vessel, any of us will encounter any life-threatening situations."

13

"You should really get your people off that ship before they end up *dead*."

The man sitting in Mitchell's command chair who called himself God was tall, with jet black hair and sharp, pointed features. He was dressed in a Fleet uniform with the rank equivalent of admiral on his badge. He sat in the command chair with the casual familiarity of an individual who was used to being at the top of the food chain. An eyebrow went up as he pressed the palms of his hands together, watching Mitchell, as he waited for the obvious response.

"Who the hell are you and how did you get on my ship?" Mitchell demanded.

The man in the command chair frowned. "That's not the obvious response."

"Somebody get security up here immediately," Mitchell said. Behind him, Zemble got up from his seat.

"Did I stuttered?" the man in the command chair asked. "Am I not speaking your language correctly? It didn't strike me as an overly complicated form of communication, but then sometimes even the simplest of things can be messed up in execution." He paused and asked, "But really, I don't think I messed this up. This is your language, yes?" He pointed to his mouth. "These words that are coming out of my mouth, you understand them? Say something that acknowledges you hear and understand me. Preferably something along the lines of, 'I hear and understand you.'"

Mitchell stepped down from the small raised platform that surrounded the bridge and approached the man in his chair. "I asked you a question."

"And I gave you a friendly little warning," the man replied. "If we're taking score, I think mine outweighs yours."

Mitchell looked over at Zemble. "Mr. Zemble, please take this man into custody."

"Yes, sir," Zemble replied.

"Really? We're going to do *this*?" the man in the command chair asked. "Really?"

Zemble pulled a fusion pistol from a hidden clutch on the side of his console.

The man in the command chair clapped with unrestrained glee. "Oh, this is going to be *delightful*, isn't it. Tell me something, how exactly do you plan to restrain *God*? Really, I want to know."

"I don't know what you are, but you are certainly not God," Zemble said.

"Oh? Really? Are you sure about that?" Suddenly there was a threatening edge to the man's voice. He leaned forward. "I mean, are you *really* sure about that?"

There was a low growl from the back of Zemble's throat as he approached the man in the command chair.

"Fair enough, I suppose," the man replied. "But, consider this counterargument."

Zemble disappeared.

Calloway gave a startled scream.

"*What the hell?!*" Rabkin exclaimed.

Mitchell turned on the man in the command chair. "What did you do?"

"I took the opportunity to remind a lesser being that he shouldn't go around trying to provoke a being from a higher dimension." The man settled back in the command chair with an air of indifference. "I like to think of it as a teachable moment. I *know*. It seems like an *obvious* thing to have to explain." He shrugged. "But some people just need things spelled out for them. Irritating, yes, but at this point I'm used to it. Seriously, though, Captain." He turned the command chair around to face the viewscreen. "You really do want to get your people off that ship as quickly as possible."

Mitchell stepped between the man and the viewscreen. "What did you do to Zemble?"

"Really? Are we still on *this*?" The man sighed and rolled his eyes. "He's not *dead*, if that's what you're worried about. Although, that would be *hilarious*, given the fact that I've warned you *twice* already about bringing your people back from that *deathtrap* over there and you just keep *ignoring* me."

"If he's not dead, then where is he?" Mitchell demanded.

"He's someplace *else*," the man replied. "Someplace where he's learning a valuable life lesson. Don't worry, I'll bring him back in one piece. More or less."

"Bring him back *now*."

The man frowned. "Captain, I don't think you understand your situation here."

"I understand that a hostile entity has boarded my ship and kidnapped one of my people," Mitchell snapped.

The man held a hand to his chest in mock outrage. "Hostile entity? *Me*? Is that how you see *me*? Captain Mitchell, I'm here to *help* you."

"You can start by returning my crewman," Mitchell said.

The man sighed again. "Fine. I can see you're just not going to let this go. Very well. Here's your little devil man back."

The man in the command chair snapped his fingers and Zemble reappeared in the exact spot he had disappeared from.

Zemble collapsed to his knees. His normally dark red skin was almost pink and his eyes were bulging from their sockets as his hands clutched at his throat.

Rabkin rushed forward, grabbing an emergency medical scanner.

Zemble made a weird gurgling noise from the back of his throat. He stared off at nothing in particular, almost as though he was unable to focus on anything.

"There you go," the man in the command chair said. "As good as new."

"His heart rate is so damn elevated it's about to explode out his damn chest," Rabkin growled.

The man in the command chair shrugged. "Like I said, I'd bring him back in one piece, more or less."

"Get me two orderlies and a gurney up here ASAP," Rabkin barked at Calloway.

"Mr. Zemble?" Mitchell asked, kneeling down in front of him. "Mr. Zemble, can you hear me?"

"I wouldn't bother," the man in the command chair said. "He's not going to be good for anything other than drooling for the next hour or so. You try talking to him before then and you'll just be wasting your time. Of course, it is *your* time to waste."

Mitchell stood up and turned to him. "What did you do?"

"How many times am I going to have to explain myself?"

"Once would be nice."

The man in the command chair clapped his hands together. "Captain. You're. Not. *Listening.*"

"And you're not listening to me," Mitchell snapped. "If you don't start explaining who the hell you are, what the hell you're doing here and how the hell you got on my ship, I'm going to send every damn security officer I have at you."

The man's face darkened. "That's going to be quite an effort in futility."

"It's my effort to be futile in," Mitchell replied.

A broad grin broke out across the man's face. "That is certainly true. Okay, fine. Let's do it your way." He paused and cleared his throat. "Once again, I'm *God*. How did I get on your ship? I *walked* here. And why am I here?" He pointed to the vessel on the viewscreen. "To warn you to get your people off that ship before it becomes their permanent resting place."

The lift opened and two orderlies stepped out onto the bridge with a gurney. They hoisted Zemble onto it with a little bit of effort.

"Get him down to sickbay and hook him up with a primary oxygen stimulant," Rabkin said.

"You go with him," Mitchell said, not taking his eyes off the man in the command chair.

"The hell I will," Rabkin started.

"That's not a suggestion, Doctor," Mitchell said. "I'm ordering you to attend to Lieutenant Zemble personally and right now."

Rabkin looked as though he was going to argue the

point one more time, but then he turned and followed the orderlies back on to the lift.

"I hope that wasn't for my benefit," the man in the command chair said. "Because it wasn't as impressive as you think it was."

Mitchell didn't say anything for a moment. He studied the man in his command chair, trying to get a read on him.

"Who the hell are you?" Mitchell asked again.

"How many times are we going to cover this?" the man replied.

"You're certainly not God," Mitchell said.

The man's gaze narrowed. "Are you *sure* you want to go down that path, Captain? Considering what just happened to your crewman?"

Mitchell looked around his bridge at his crew. They ranged from tense to scared.

He looked at the man in his chair and said evenly, "God doesn't just show up and scare his people half to death."

"Sure He does," the man said. "Haven't you ever read the Bible? That's basically the entire Old Testament. I'm pretty sure if I was a simple-minded human being such as yourself I would have found the parting of the Red Sea rather shit-inducing." He paused and then added, "As I would have shat my pants at the sight of it." He tilted his head to the side. "Well, robes, I suppose. They hadn't really invented pants yet at that point, had they?"

"You would know," Mitchell said. "Since you're supposed to be God."

The man smiled. "Oh, is that supposed to be cleverness on your part? Trying to trip me up? Trap me in my own words?"

Mitchell didn't respond to that.

The man in the command chair bristled with impatience. "*Fine*." He held out his hands, spreading them wide. "I'm a being from a higher dimension. How high you might ask? Well, let's say it's the kind of dimension that looks down on your dimension in the same way you look at words on a piece of paper. What can you do to those words? *Anything you want*. Because they're *words*, on a piece of *paper*." He pointed at Mitchell. "That's what you are to me. So, with that in mind, what would *you* call *me*? Because from where I'm sitting, God seems pretty all-encompassing." He sat back in the command chair with a smug look on his face. "I won't lie, Captain, I'm rather impressed with myself. It's not an easy thing to distill the particulars of life as being from a higher dimension into an analogy that's easily digested by simple being such as yourself. But I think I just did a hell of a job."

He looked around the bridge. "Anybody care to give me a round of applause?" He waited for a moment. "No? Well, I believe your Nikola Tesla wasn't appreciated in his time either."

"I can't call you God," Mitchell said.

"Sure you can," the man in the command chair replied, studying his nails. "It's easy. Three letters, one word, at the front of every sentence."

"I *won't* call you God," Mitchell clarified.

He looked up from his nails. "Well, there we go." He took a moment, scrunching his face up in an exaggerated expression of thought and then said, "Fine. Why don't we go with Steve?"

Mitchell blinked, thrown off his guard "…Steve?"

The man in the command chair shrugged. "Sure, why not? It's as good a name as any. It certainly doesn't have the same panache as God. But then, what does?"

"That's not your real name."

"Well, of course it isn't," he said, as if he was speaking

to a child. "Do I look like an entity who was conceived as a *Steve*?"

"Then why…?"

He sighed impatiently again. "Because I don't really care what you call me. But you clearly need to call me *something* and I don't think you'll agree to calling me with God with a little 'g.'

"Because this is what my real name looks like." He waved his hand and $12 > 19\%/(89^2)^0$ appeared in the air between them. "Do you know how to pronounce that in your language? Because I'm a being from a much higher plane of existence and even *I* don't know how to do that." He waved his hand again as if wiping away the formula and it disappeared.

"And finally, because I'm not here to quibble with you about my *damn name*." He pointed over Mitchell's shoulder at the ship on the viewscreen. "I'm here to tell you to get your people off that *damn ship*."

To his credit, Mitchell remained unfazed. "You've got a funny way of passing along a warning."

"I'm known across the multiverse for my sense of humor," Steve replied flatly. "To be fair, I did consider just leaving you a mysterious note lying around, but you people struck me as needing a personal touch. Also, full disclosure, I don't have the greatest penmanship. It's a dying art everywhere."

Mitchell stepped to the left side of the chair and Steve slowly swiveled to follow him.

"What's wrong with that ship?" Mitchell asked.

"You mean other than the obvious?" Steve replied. "Please, Captain, don't tell me you're *that* dense."

"It's a dead ship." Mitchell looked at Sadler.

"The only lifeforms our sensors are picking up is our away team," she said.

Steve clapped his hands together. "Oh, well, in that case, clearly I'm *mistaken*. I don't know what I was thinking. After all, I'm just a being from a higher dimension with a greater wealth of knowledge regarding how the very nature of reality works, so naturally I don't know what I'm talking about." Steve swiveled the command chair around to face Sadler. "Tell me, Ms. Sadler, how many different forms of life are you familiar with?"

"I'm sorry?" Sadler asked.

"What the hell is wrong with you people?" Steve asked. "Is there something in the way I present my questions that immediately confounds you?" He took a deep breath and said again, slower this time, "How many different forms of life are you familiar with?"

Sadler didn't answer. Instead, she looked at Mitchell. "Captain?"

Mitchell shook his head. "Don't worry about it, Commander."

Steve turned to Mitchell. "It's a fairly relevant question. After all, you're only going to look for what you're familiar with. If you're not aware of it, how do you know to look for it?"

"Are you saying there's something on that ship?" Mitchell asked.

"I'm saying you need to get your people off there before you find out."

"Why?"

"Because it's my understanding that in this lower dimension, you aren't fond of your fellow beings dying because you did something *stupid*." Steve leaned forward. "Tell me, Captain Gavin Mitchell of the *USS Defiance*, tell me what about a human vessel appearing this far out, transmitting a code that's nearly four hundred years old, doesn't strike you as suspiciously *problematic*?" He raised both eyebrows. "It's a damn *trap* and I'm just sitting here wondering how in all the multiverse you're too *dumb* to see that."

"A mystery isn't the same as a trap," Mitchell replied.

"That's what the fool says when he's too foolish to realize that the trap has already been sprung."

Mitchell looked at Steve gravely. "I don't know a damn thing about you. So I don't know why you would you think I wouldn't take anything you say with anything less than a grain of salt."

"Because in addition to simply appearing on your vessel out in the middle of space, I figured snapping away your crewman to another dimension and making symbols appear in thin air would prove my bona fides," Steve replied.

"All that proves is that you're a powerful and dangerous entity," Mitchell said.

"That doesn't mean I'm wrong."

"What do you want?" Mitchell asked.

"Nothing that you can provide," Steve replied.

"Then what the hell are you doing here?"

"Just trying to save you a lot of trouble. Obviously, you're not interested."

"You haven't given me anything more a vague warning," Mitchell said.

"I don't think so. Telling you to get your people off that deathtrap sounds pretty specific to me." Steve looked around the bridge. "Anyone else around here find that 'vague'?"

"Don't talk to my crew," Mitchell said.

Steve turned back to Mitchell. "I'm not here for what you people call a 'pissing contest.' The *Eternal Hand of God* has been bait for some time now and I've seen quite a few species board that vessel thinking all the same things you are. You know what happened to them? They're all dead."

"Why didn't you warn them?"

"I did," Steve said. "They didn't listen either."

"Whose trap is it?" Mitchell asked.

"Who do you think?"

"I don't know."

Steve rolled his eyes dramatically. "Take your best guess. It can be as wild as you want it to be and I can almost guarantee you'll get it right. Because you cannot possibly be that dumb."

Mitchell didn't respond.

"Sure." Steve sighed again. He held his hands up, palms out. "Can't say I didn't warn you."

And then he disappeared.

14

"WHAT THE HELL was that all about?" Warrick asked, glancing down as Nax disconnected from the open channel back to the *Defiance*.

"Apparently they had a visitor," Nax replied, squinting at the light from Warrick that was now in his face.

Warrick moved his flashlight so it wasn't shining directly in Nax's eyes, but didn't budge from his spot. He stared down at his friend, his mouth agape. "I beg your frackin' pardon?"

"According to the captain, an entity of unknown origin appeared on the ship, attacked Zemble, warned the captain that we should leave this vessel immediately and then promptly disappeared."

"What the hell does that mean?" Warrick asked. "Disappeared? The hell?"

Nax shifted his weight uncomfortably as he clung to the ladder. It was covered in the same crumbly space dust as the rest of the ship. "You know as much as I know at this point, Jaxson. Can we please continue? This is far from a comfortable position to maintain while having this conversation."

Warrick shook his head and started back up the ladder. "Disappeared? Who just disappears? There aren't any secret passageways off the bridge." He paused and then added, "Well, at least there's nothing big enough for a person to slip through."

"When the captain explained that this entity disappeared he made it very clear that he meant it in the most literal way possible," Nax replied, following up after his friend.

"One does not simply disappear," Askon said from beneath them.

"That's what I'm trying to say," Warrick said.

"The Gibrilia have the illusion of disappearing from sight," Askon continued. "But that's a trick due to the hallucinogenic pheromones they excrete. Was it a Gibrilian, Commander?"

"If it was a Gibrilian, I believe the captain would have said so," Nax replied.

"Also there's no way in hell that a Gibrilian could make it this far out," Warrick said. "Don't they only have a lifespan of six months?"

"That is true," Askon agreed.

"They also smell like Emhea horse shit," Warrick said. "That odor of theirs gets everywhere. If there was a damn Gibrilian on the *Defiance* we would have smelled it a while ago."

"As fascinating as that sounds," Nax said. "I would like to point out that the captain was very clear that it was an *unknown* entity."

"Hang on," Warrick said, stopping next to a door on his left. "I think we're here." He looped his arm around the railing of the ladder and pulled out his datapad for reference. He scanned the blueprint and then looked at the closed door. The symbol, two circles standing on top of each other with three parallel lines crossing through their center, matched the same one on the datapad. He dropped the pad back into his workbag and pulled out a photon wrench. "Yeah, this is definitely it."

Warrick located something that looked like a control box and used the photon wrench to pop open the panel.

"Perhaps our initial sensor sweeps missed a possible lifeform on this vessel?" Askon suggested. "A ship of this size, with as much particle decay as it has apparently suffered over the last few centuries, it is certainly possible our sensors could have missed something. They are not as fine-tuned as other UPA ships."

"Considering what I have to work with," Warrick said, studying the wires inside the control box, "our sensors are practically award-winning." He reached in and yanked out a handful of the wires.

"I, of course, meant no disrespect, Commander," Askon said.

"Sure you didn't," Warrick said, stripping several of the wires. He touched a few of them together. Nothing happened. "That's why you keep filing work requests with my department to overhaul the sensor array."

Nax cleared his throat loudly.

Warrick rolled his eyes. "Fine. Let's say we missed something." He replaced the wrench with a pulse spanner and reached deeper into the control box. "How did it get from here to the *Defiance*?"

"Obviously if we missed its life signs, we could have missed a shuttle or some other small craft that deployed from the *Eternal Hand of God*," Askon said.

"If the *Defiance* had been boarded by another vessel I

would believe that the captain would have led with that," Nax said. "Captain Mitchell implied some form of tele-portation."

Warrick stopped what he was doing and stared down at Nax.

Nax pulled his hand from the ladder to block the light from Warrick's flashlight again. "I am simply relaying what the captain told me, Jaxson." He spoke with the tired sigh of a man used to having an endless familiar argument.

"Am I missing something?" Askon asked.

"Commander Warrick is not fond of Gunning's Theory of Spatial Manipulation," Nax said.

"Because it's not a damn theory of anything. It's basi-cally bloody *magic*. That's what it is," Warrick said, turning back to the control box. He found what felt like a fuse switch buried at the back of the control box. He tried to position his flashlight to get an actual look at it, but it was nearly impossible to maneuver the flashlight close enough to the box without letting go of the ladder and plunging into the darkness below.

So Warrick did the next best thing. He wrapped his fingers around the fuse switch and yanked it out.

There was a soft *clunk* and the door opened about two inches.

Warrick pulled his hand from the control box and grabbed the edge of the door closest to him and pulled it open the rest of the way.

A few minutes later all three men were out of the conduit tube and on the floor of a deck.

"It's hardly magic," Nax said, waving his flashlight around the dark corridor. It didn't appear to be any different from the deck they had just climbed up from. Although, the darkness didn't help.

"Sure it is. That's what you call something that sure as

hell isn't science," Warrick said, brushing the dust from his uniform. He held up the fuse switch for a closer look under his flashlight. It was square shaped with three copper-colored prongs extending from the top and bottom. He touched one of the prongs with his pinky. Despite its smooth appearance, there was a coarseness to it. "Hell, I can sit around in my office and come up with all sorts of half-assed theories for things that can't possibly be done. Here, I'll come up with one right now. Base atomic particle manipulation: reorganizing the basic atomic structure of an item so that it becomes a completely different item. Can I prove that it's possible? Of course not. You try to reorganize the atomic structure of any one particular item and you'll either blow up the damn thing or turn it into sludge."

"Either way," Askon said, looking up from his scanner, "you've effectively changed its base atomic structure, essentially proving your theory true."

Warrick glared at Askon.

"Obviously you haven't transformed it into anything useful," Askon added. "But on a basic technical level, you've proven your theory is possible."

"That doesn't change the fact that teleportation isn't a real thing," Warrick said, dropping the fuse switch into his workbag. "You can theorize about it all you want, it's not going to make it any more real than a six-breasted Faulir."

Askon raised a slender finger. "Except that on Nion Twenty-Seven scientists managed to transport one atom from one side of the planet to the other through spatial manipulation."

Warrick pulled out his datapad back out to consult the map. "Well now, that changes *everything*, doesn't it? One damn atom gets moved around and suddenly we're just 'porting people all over the galaxy."

"Hardly, Commander," Askon said.

"*Exactly*." As he powered up the datapad, Warrick noticed that Nax hadn't been a part of the conversation for the last few minutes. "Nax? You still with us?"

Nax's eyes blinked rapidly as he turned away from the darkness he had been staring into and readjusted themselves to the dim lighting of their flashlights. "I'm sorry?"

Warrick frowned and walked over to his friend. "You okay?"

"I am perfectly fine," Nax replied, taking a deep breath.

Warrick glanced at Askon, but he was distracted by the readings on his scanner. "You don't look fine," he said to Nax in a voice low enough for just the two of them.

Nax waved him off. "I am simply a little winded from our climb up here."

"Sure," Warrick said, not sounding very convinced. "Don't think I didn't notice whatever that was back at the airlock."

"I'm not certain I know what you're talking about," Nax said carefully.

Warrick gave him a look, but didn't say anything. Instead he turned his attention back to his datapad. "I heard what happened on the bridge."

"How close are we to engineering?" Nax asked, attempting to change the conversation.

"Not close enough," Warrick replied. He double checked their route and then pointed to their left. "That way." He slipped the datapad back into his workbag. "When were you going to tell me you haven't been sleeping?"

Nax waved his light in the direction Warrick pointed. "As soon as it became apparent that it was necessary to do so."

"What the hell is that supposed to mean?" Warrick asked. He tried to meet Nax's eyes, but the helmsman avoided his gaze. "Hey, look, I can't help you if you don't keep me in the loop."

"I assure you, you are definitely in the loop."

Warrick didn't look convinced. He glanced Askon's way to make sure he still wasn't paying any attention to their conversation. The Knok was focused intently on something on the wall.

Warrick turned back to Nax. "You were out of it for a couple of days there."

"Yes, I am aware of that," Nax replied.

"Practically catatonic."

"I wouldn't go that far."

"I would," Warrick said. "Who are you trying to fool? Because it sure as hell ain't me."

Nax just raised a hairless eyebrow in response.

"Oh, sure, you've got your composure down to a science," Warrick said. "Practically a damn art form at this point. But you're about two seconds away from cracking."

Nax frowned. "I'm not going to crack."

"I've heard about the wailing," Warrick said.

Nax didn't have a response to that.

"You didn't think I wasn't going to hear about it?"

"I did not say that."

"No, but you were sure as hell thinking it."

"I am simply attempting to process my grief," Nax said.

Warrick stared at him for a moment, trying to search his face for something. He shook his head. "I wish that was the truth."

Nax's brow furrowed slightly.

Warrick sighed. "You going to take a nap when we get back to the ship?"

"I'm not certain what that has to do with our current situation."

"Are you going to take a nap when we get back to the ship?" Warrick repeated.

Nax exhaled slowly. "As long as the captain no longer has any need of my services for the time being, I will certainly make every effort to do just that," he said. "However, I wouldn't characterize myself as feeling optimistic in the outcome."

"Uh-huh."

"I'm sorry if you were expecting something a little more dramatic." Nax waved his light at Askon. "Lieutenant? Have you found something of note?"

Warrick hesitated for a moment before following Nax over to Askon. He glanced back in the direction Nax had been staring in. The beam of his flashlight didn't illuminate anything interesting. He didn't bother to pull out his scanner and check for any life signs nearby. He had been in space long enough to know when they were alone.

Askon was examining a thin red line across the wall under the glow of his light. "Some sort of synium mold property."

Warrick walked over and leaned in for a closer look. "Space mold?"

Askon gently pushed the chief engineer back. "I wouldn't get that close to it. It's composed of microscopic spores that could possibly cause internal hemorrhaging if inhaled."

Warrick took a step back, holding a hand across his mouth. "Right. Good save."

"I've never seen anything quite like it before," Askon continued. "For all intents and purposes, it's nearly identical to mold native to Earth."

"I don't recall Earth having any mold that could cause instant internal hemorrhaging," Warrick said.

"Nearly identical," Askon said. "It has three additional genetic markers not found in any variety on Earth."

"And elsewhere?" Nax asked.

Askon's antennae twitched back and forth. "Not that my scanner is familiar with. I'd like to take a sample back to the Defiance for further testing."

Nax nodded his assent.

Askon pulled out a small tube and gently scraped a sample of the red space mold into it before sealing it shut.

Warrick pointed off into the darkness. "Engineering's that way." He paused and then pointed his light up towards the ceiling. "Actually, I think it's that way. But the access tube we need to get up there is that way." He pointed down the hallway.

"More climbing?" Askon's antennae drooped slightly.

"Hopefully I can get some basic power back up and it'll be a shorter trip back to the shuttle," Warrick said. He looked at Nax. "Although, I'm not optimistic."

Nax didn't bother to reply to that.

Warrick pointed back to the tube they just came out of. "According to the map, that tube back there was sealed off due to a hull breach two decks up."

Askon's antennae twitched nervously. "Are we going to be able to gain access to engineering?"

Warrick nodded. "I think so." He pointed with his chin in the direction they were supposed to go. "This route should take us around the breach. All the containment systems still seem to be operating just fine, seeing as we're not standing in the middle of a vacuum right now. Hopefully with main power or even emergency power, I can get some lifts running around here. That should cut down on any climbing after that."

"Then lead us on, Jaxson," Nax said, gesturing towards the dark corridor before them. When he was certain Warrick was no longer paying any attention, he glanced back into the darkness behind them.

The haunting spectral image of Grace Hawkins no longer lingered there.

15

THE FIRST SKELETON they came across put to rest any question as to what species the former occupants of the *Eternal Hand of God* were.

"Human." Dheer crouched over the remains in the wide tunnel. Her medical scanner verified it, but she didn't need it to. She was all too familiar with what the human skeleton looked like. Even one that was missing its skull and was, according to her scanner, over three hundred years old.

Grell picked up a bone and it immediately crumbled in his hand.

Dheer shot him a look. "I shouldn't have to tell you not to do that."

"Sorry," Grell said with a sheepish look.

The tunnel Warrick had directed them to was huge. Easily seventy feet in diameter. There were four tracks spaced evenly apart along the curved walls of the tunnel. An ambient light source hidden along the top of the tunnel cast the space in a dim, pale glow. Not bright enough to illuminate the entire tunnel, but enough for the team to put their flashlights away.

"Three hundred years," Keane said, shaking his head. "Shit. We were just barely out of our solar system. When did Earth get into the UPA? Twenty-three hundred?"

"We petitioned for membership in Twenty-Two-Oh-Six," Grell answered. "And we were granted probationary status in Twenty-Two-Ten and became full members in Twenty-Two-Twenty."

Keane looked at him, surprised.

"What?" Grell asked. "I like history."

"What do you think he died of?" Keane asked.

Dheer looked at him out of the corner of her eye.

"Obviously it wasn't old age," Keane added.

"Your deductive skills remain unparalleled," Dheer said, standing up. She gestured at the skeleton. "I couldn't even begin to guess what killed him." She carefully stepped around to the top of the skeleton in order to see if she could find the missing skull. But there was no sign of it. "There doesn't seem to be any signs of blunt force trauma." She shrugged. "Maybe it was old age."

Keane did not look impressed.

"I'm not a forensic specialist," Dheer said. "You got a broken bone, I can fix it. You want me to study some bones and figure out what killed their owner? Go find somebody else."

"Yeah, you've definitely been hanging around Rabkin too much," Keane said.

Dheer rubbed her forehead tiredly. "No argument there."

Keane looked around the massive tunnel. "There's no way this ship is one of ours."

Dheer started moving back down the tunnel. "And yet, this was clearly a human body."

"You ever seen this kind of design structure on a UPA vessel?" Keane asked, following her and Grell. "Human or otherwise? I don't think Warrick's even seen anything like this before."

"I don't know what you want me to say, Cayden," Dheer said. "You're the one who was all excited about a space mystery."

Keane gestured back to the skeleton. "I mean, how did he even get out here?"

"Probably the same way the rest of us did," Dheer said.

Keane started to say something else, but the words didn't make it out of his mouth.

Nobody spoke for the next ten minutes or so. It was hard to find anything to say.

After the first skeleton, more started slowly appearing along their path. Each one in an extreme state of decay. Most of them were human. Some of them weren't. Occasionally there would be an alien skeletal structure Dheer was familiar with: Phaw, Elwat, and even a Veneer. But more often than not, the alien skeletons mixed in with the human were far outside her realm of expertise. Colors, shapes and structures she had never even read about.

And each one was missing its skull.

After a while, Dheer stopped with the pretense of scanning them. The results were all the same: Whoever these people were, they were long, long dead.

But it wasn't so much the loosely formed skeletons littering their path that gave the away team pause, as it was the fact that at some point in the past, the bodies had clearly been moved along the farthest edges of the tunnel, creating a well-defined path for the away team to follow.

The path was well worn. They weren't the first to

follow it and the footsteps they followed in were clearly long before their time.

They were each thinking the same things: What had happened on this ship and who else had walked this path before them?

And the one question that neither one of them wanted to ask out loud: what happened to all the skulls?

As they neared the end of the tunnel, something off the beaten path caught Keane's eye. The dim lighting of the tunnel glinted off a piece of metal that looked vaguely familiar.

"Hang on," he said to Dheer and Grell, who were both a few steps ahead of him.

Carefully, using his cane to push some of the skeletons out of his way, Keane waded into the pile of bones. It wasn't far.

Beneath the discolored ribcage of an individual who had probably been dead since long before the Alliance had any inclination of sending ships out this far, Keane picked up a swatch of cloth with a very familiar metal shape.

Keane turned around and held it up for the other two to see.

It was a black onyx UPA badge.

16

"Well?" Mitchell asked, his arms folded as he stood in the doorway of Rabkin's office.

Rabkin pushed past him, peeling off his gloves and tossing them in a sanitizing receptacle on the other side of the room. "Unconscious, but stable." He dropped into his seat behind his desk with a tired sigh.

"What happened?" Sadler asked. She sat across from Rabkin.

"Hell if I know," Rabkin said. He rubbed a hand over the side of his face. "His body shows all the signs of extreme oxygen deprivation."

"I don't like that look on your face, old man," Mitchell said.

Rabkin grunted. "You're going to like this even less. According to my exam, and this is my best guess estimate, Zemble wasn't breathing for the better part of an hour, possibly more."

Sadler gave a low whistle.

Mitchell's expression was simmering rage. "How the hell is he even still alive?"

Rabkin held up his hands in defeat. "Your guess is as good as mine. Here's a fun fact about Elwats: They have terrible lung capacity. The longest any Elwat has been able to hold his or her breath is six minutes. That's less than half the average in the UPA. You're right. Zemble should be dead right now. I don't know why the hell he is isn't and that's pissing me off."

"Anything else?"

Rabkin shook his head. "His body's clean. Too clean, in fact. I could send him through our decontaminate sanitizer and he wouldn't come out this clean."

"So what happened to him?" Mitchell asked.

"Hell if I know."

"Where'd he go?"

"Copy and paste my last answer here."

"Damnit, Jim," Mitchell snapped.

Rabkin held up his hands for Mitchell to calm down. "Hold your damn horses, Gavin. I'm not the bad guy here. I'm just telling you what I found."

"Which is *nothing*."

"Sure," Rabkin said. "It's not great. But let me tell you, if you're looking for how to suffocate an Elwat and keep him alive, you don't have a lot of options available to you."

"Which means?"

Rabkin shrugged. "Well, you've heard the expression that there's more than one way to skin a cat?" He pointed out to the main med bay where Zemble was resting. "I can sure as promise you're not going to find more than one way to do whatever was done to him."

"If that's supposed to be comforting or inspire confidence, it's not," Mitchell said.

Rabkin shrugged again. "That's why I'm a doctor and not a greeting card writer."

"Did he regain consciousness at all?" Sadler asked.

"For a few minutes," Rabkin said. "I don't think he's aware of anything though. His pupils remained unfocused. He didn't follow any line of light and didn't seem to be aware of my voice."

Nobody spoke for a minute.

"Okay, fine, I'll ask the uncomfortable question," Mitchell said finally. "Anyone suffering from severe oxygen deprivation runs the risk of permanent brain damage. Where are Zemble's odds?"

Rabkin pursed his lips and stared down at his desk. He pushed some things around in no apparent order to tidy anything up. It was only a few seconds, but it felt longer.

Eventually, Rabkin looked back up at Mitchell, his expression severe. "I'm not going to bullshit you, Gavin. In Zemble's case, it's not great. The only other case I could find that was remotely similar to Zemble's condition, they ended up a vegetable for the rest of their natural life."

Mitchell pounded his fist against the door frame in frustration.

"If you feel so inclined, prayers wouldn't be out of the question at this point," Rabkin said.

"And who I am supposed to be praying to?" Mitchell asked. "*Steve?*"

Rabkin snorted. "If he's God then I'm a damn genie."

"Do you have another explanation for what happened?" Mitchell asked.

"No, I don't," Rabkin said. "But that doesn't mean I'm just going to dive head first into the first half-baked theory that gets conveniently dropped into my lap."

Mitchell ran his hands over his face. "Right." He turned to Sadler. "Commander?"

"Alright. So it's my turn, I guess?" Sadler crossed her legs. "Well, for starters, our sensors didn't record him coming or going. In fact, they didn't record him at all."

Rabkin raised a bushy eyebrow. "What the hell does that mean?"

"It means that when I reviewed the bridge footage from when Steve first appeared, it looks like the captain's talking to thin air," Sadler said.

Rabkin looked at Mitchell, confused and surprised.

"I'm sure it'll look great in my personnel file," Mitchell said.

"Well, I think the fact that Zemble disappears and reappears should help keep you from losing your command over any mental competency issues," Sadler said. "But whatever this Steve is, he's completely invisible to our sensors."

"That's not possible," Rabkin grumbled.

Sadler gestured to his console screen. "I can play the footage for you."

"Maybe later," Rabkin said. "I'll need a good laugh after Zemble pulls through."

Sadler turned back to Mitchell. "Not only did the sensors not record him, but like I said, we don't have any record of him boarding the *Defiance* or leaving. But it's the fact that the sensors didn't record *anything* that I find disturbing. To do whatever he did to Zemble, it should require *something*. There should be some record of at least a form of energy used to displace Zemble and there's just nothing. One second he's there, the next he isn't. Just like Steve."

Mitchell folded his arms. "Theories?"

Sadler rolled her lips together and shook her head. "Hell if I know."

"I'd like something a little more substantial than that, Commander."

"Hell if I know, *sir*."

Mitchell frowned.

Rabkin rocked back in his chair, snorting to keep from breaking out into laughter.

"It's not funny," Mitchell said.

"No, it's not," Rabkin agreed. "But the day's turning into a real shit show, so I'm taking my stress relief where I can get it."

"He said he just walked onto our ship," Mitchell said.

Sadler shrugged. "Maybe he did?"

"From where?"

"Somewhere else."

Mitchell sighed. "Commander…"

"I don't know what to tell you, Captain," Sadler said. "But I don't have a lot of experience in explaining the impossible."

"We can't take what he says at face value," Mitchell said.

"But I don't know how else to take it," Sadler said.

"Your parents are missionaries, aren't they?" Rabkin asked her.

"Yes."

"In your opinion then, what happened?" Rabkin asked.

"My *opinion*?" Sadler repeated.

"Sure. You're one of the big kids now," Rabkin said. "And let's face it, you oughta have something to bring to the table here."

"Because my parents are missionaries?" Sadler asked in an attempt to clarify.

Rabkin leaned forward, folding his hands on the desk. "Well, the man did appear out of nowhere and called himself God. That's got to count for something."

"You just said that you didn't believe him," Sadler replied.

"Sure. And I don't. That doesn't mean you're not allowed to have a differing opinion."

Sadler looked at Mitchell like she was expecting an out.

"He makes a point every now and then, " Mitchell said.

"Captain, Doctor," Sadler began. "Just because my parents are missionaries hardly makes me any kind of expert on who God is."

"If I was looking for an expert opinion I'd dial up the damn Pope," Rabkin said. "And even then, I'm not exactly sure that bastard fits the definition."

"I don't know what to tell you," Sadler said. "It's not like I had a personal relationship with God."

"Considering the circumstances, anything would be helpful at this point, Commander," Mitchell said.

Sadler took a deep breath and exhaled slowly. "Honestly? I'm not entirely certain He even exists. At least, not in the way that my parents do."

Rabkin looked at her, genuinely surprised. "Well, there's a twist I didn't see coming."

"There was an entity on my bridge that fit the standard description of God," Mitchell said.

"There's a lot of stuff in this universe that can't be explained," Sadler said. "And if there really was a God, specifically a God as my parents and so many other people believe in, how do you explain things like the Unity?"

"I believe the go-to explanation is that the Lord works in mysterious ways," Mitchell said.

"All due respect, Captain, that's not an explanation it's an excuse, " Sadler said. "Something in the universe doesn't make sense? Well, God just works in mysterious ways." She shook her head. "I'm sorry, but I don't buy that."

"Then what do you buy?" Mitchell asked.

"I don't know."

"Alright," Rabkin said. "This one's my fault. I was trying to help us find some answers and instead I steered us right into a theological debate. I don't know about either of you two, but I'm too damn old for one of those right now. They never end soon enough and I'd rather not die discussing whether or not God is real."

Mitchell nodded. "Fair enough. So what's Steve then?"

"Are either of you familiar with Captain Jedidiah Antos?" Sadler asked.

Mitchell and Rabkin exchanged a bemused look.

"Sure. Antos was famous for turning in reports that were…" Mitchell trailed off, unable to find an appropriate word to describe the reports.

"They were bullshit is what they were," Rabkin said.

"I don't know that I'd go that far," Mitchell said.

"I would," Rabkin said. "Remember the one about the giant glowing hand in space? Bullshit. Antos probably spent a damn week laughing over that one. There's a reason they stopped teaching him in the Academy. I still don't know how a clown like him got a damn command."

"It was a different time back then," Mitchell said. "Seventy-five years ago. Things were still a mess after the Irac Conflict. The Fleet made all sorts of decisions in order to keep things together."

Rabkin grunted his disagreement.

"So, about seventy-two years ago," Sadler continued. "The *Kirkland* had an encounter with an unknown entity that displayed abilities very similar to our friend Steve."

"What happened?" Mitchell asked.

"According to the ship's logs, the *Kirkland* was transporting medical supplies to Brovkin Six," Sadler said.

"About two hours out from orbit they came into contact with an entity who went by the name Zeus."

"Zeus?" Rabkin repeated. "*Zeus*. I call bullshit. Bull. *Shit*."

"In Captain Antos' report, he claimed that the entity manifested himself on the bridge of the *Kirkland* and introduced himself as the Mad God Zeus."

Both of Rabkin's bushy eyebrows went up and he looked at Mitchell. "This is why nobody liked Antos."

"The man legitimately pioneered several advanced forms of spaceship combat," Mitchell said.

"He was also a massive asshole," Rabkin said. "You need to pick better role models."

"You're a pretty big asshole yourself," Mitchell pointed out.

"Sure," he agreed. "But I don't go around submitting reports back to Fleet Command about how I'm running into Greek gods roaming space. I limit the extent of my assholeness."

Mitchell looked at Sadler. "Commander," he said, prompting her to continue.

"Well, Zeus transported the entire crew of the *Kirkland* into a facsimile of an ancient Roman colosseum where they were forced into combat against unknown alien creatures."

"Can't even get his damn references right," Rabkin grumbled.

"How the hell did he do that?" Mitchell asked.

Sadler shrugged. "How did Steve transport Zemble to an unknown location where he didn't breathe and then bring him back?"

"Hang on," Rabkin said, holding up his hand. "Let's not get distracted here. I want to know what happened to the crew of the *Kirkland*."

"I thought you thought it was bullshit?" Mitchell asked.

"I do," Rabkin said. "That doesn't mean I don't want to know how it ends. Antos was an asshole, but he knew how to spin a damn good story."

"Well, most of them made it back to the *Kirkland*," Sadler said. "According to the captain's logs, they lost six officers, but were able to still deliver the medical supplies to the colony on Brovkin IV."

Rabkin shook his head. "Nope. There's got to be more to the story. You're leaving out a pretty big chunk there. This is Jedidiah Antos. How the hell did they get one over on this Mad God Zeus?"

Sadler hesitated for a moment, looking back and forth between Mitchell and Rabkin. "They…didn't. Captain Antos wrote that during his match, Zeus was confronted by another, apparently similar being, and was…chastised."

"I beg your damn pardon?" Rabkin asked. "What the hell do you mean he was 'chastised.'"

Sadler shifted in her seat, an awkward, uncomfortable grin on her face. "The second being identified itself as Zeus' mother."

Rabkin smacked his desk. "Now I *know* you're bullshitting me."

Sadler held up her hands. "I'm just telling you what was in the reports. Zeus' mother intervened and returned the crew of the *Kirkland* back to their ship. Various personal logs reported they were away for days, but according to the ship's internal logs, no one ever left."

"Like I said," Rabkin grunted. "Bullshit."

"The six dead crewman were still dead upon their return," Sadler said. "And according to the autopsies on file, their causes of death were consistent with reports of how they died."

Rabkin folded his arms and sat back in his chair. "Bullshit."

Sadler shrugged.

"What happened?" Mitchell asked.

"Well, as you both already pointed out, half the Fleet thought it was a joke," Sadler replied. "The other half thought the crew of the *Kirkland* went space crazy for a few days. Either way, nobody actually believed they ran into a godlike being and his mother. Still, the six dead crewmen were hard to explain."

"Was there ever an explanation?" Mitchell asked.

Sadler shook her head. "Captain Antos stood by every word he wrote in his reports until the day he died."

"Sure he did," Rabkin said. "Because he was a damn asshole. If he recanted anything in those reports they probably would have made him give back one of the damn medals they kept showering him with."

"Any other similar incidents outside of what happened with the *Kirkland*?" Mitchell asked.

Sadler shook her head. "No."

"Not much of lead there," Rabkin said.

"Steve implied that we should know who the *Eternal Hand of God* belongs to," Mitchell said. "Any theories as to what he meant?"

"Actually, yes." Sadler reached across Rabkin's desk and called up an image of a black onyx UPA badge. "Keane sent this along a little while ago. They found it on the ship."

"Black badge used to be Security and Tactical Division," Mitchell said. "Hasn't been used in the last hundred years, though. What the hell is it doing on that ship?"

"Well, there was a serial number on the back and guess where it led to?" Sadler swiped to the next screen and a photo of a man in his late twenties appeared. "Lieutenant

Commander Cory Mongan. He was an officer on the *Columbia* a hundred years ago."

"Shit," Mitchell swore under his breath as he saw where this was going.

"Lieutenant Commander Mongan, along with the other three hundred souls on the *Columbia* were killed in action one hundred years ago during the initial attack by the Unity."

17

"Bloody hell." Warrick's voice sounded muffled from inside the open floor panel.

The engineering department of the *Eternal Hand of God* was surprisingly cramped, considering the size of the ship and its massive open spaces.

There was a sunken ceiling that threatened to crack open at any given moment.

Most of the consoles were not only dead, they were covered in scorch marks or were wrecked completely, as if a massive explosion had torn through the department.

The main engine coils were dormant and cold to the touch.

The air was stale and flat. It tickled the back of Warrick's throat every time he breathed too deeply.

"Excuse me, Commander?" Askon said, bouncing his light across the cramped space and back to the chief engineer. He squatted over a large pile of gel packs on the floor. In fact, much of the floor was covered in gel packs. Almost every pack was filled with a similar, goo-like substance. In some packs, it was a dark green. In most though, it had a grayish appearance as though all the color had been completely drained.

Warrick pulled his head out from the hole in the floor. His face was covered in dust and dirt. He squinted under the beam from "I said, 'Bloody hell.'" He wiped a sleeve across his face.

"I'm afraid I don't follow."

"There are pipelines running underneath," Warrick said, getting to his feet. He tapped his toes against the floor panels. "Massive pipelines all running from the main engines." He nodded at the giant coils that, in the dim lighting of their flashlights, rose up ominously into the sunken ceiling, giving the impression that the coils were two massive hands generated by the ship itself to keep the ceiling from collapsing on them. "It funnels the power from the main engines throughout the rest of the ship. Not a damn scratch on them. Over five hundred years old and they practically look brand new. Or, at least, whatever passes for brand new back when they built this heap."

He reached into his workbag and pulled out a handful of glow sticks. With a quick twist, the sticks started glowing a bright, neon green and Warrick started tossing them around haphazardly. Slowly, the immediate area was cast in neon green light.

Warrick sighed, scratching the back of his head as he stared at the piles of gel packs scattered across the floor. Something was bugging him, but he couldn't quite put his finger on it.

Like the rest of the ship they had trekked through, the walls were covered in the thick space dust. Here, though, it created illusions of stalagmites extending down from the drooping ceiling and the pylons that crisscrossed above them.

Askon picked up one of the gel packs that still had

some color in it. "This is rather remarkable. My scanner's picking up almost fifteen terajoules of power from this pack alone."

Warrick made his way over to a console that appeared less scorched than the others. He set his workbag down. "Like I said, they're very effective. The real question is, what the hell are they doing on the damn floor?"

Warrick opened a side panel on the console and immediately started cursing in Vulderran. While the surface of the console was relatively unscathed, its interior was a mess of cables and wires that were either cut, stripped or frayed apart.

"What seems to be the problem?" Askon asked.

Warrick didn't answer him. Instead he moved to another console, this one adjacent to the main engines, and quickly opened it up. Inside he found a scene that matched the other console. Warrick looked around engineering again. All the damage was taking on a very different look now.

Warrick shook his head. "None of this makes any damn sense." He pointed to the gel packs. "Those don't belong there and those," he turned and pointed to the mess inside both consoles, "shouldn't look like a skinless Gaqex weasel built a nest in there." He nodded at the scorch marks along the other consoles. "And look at the damn scorch pattern on those. Who the hell in their right mind fires a damn fusion weapon less than ten feet from the main engine?"

Askon's antennae twitched and turned in opposite directions. "I doubt an invading party would be terribly concerned about where they would be using their weapons."

"They ought to be," Warrick said. He pointed to the main engine coils. "One stray blast and the whole ship would go up like a Valmoin supernova. *That's* the real problem with the gel packs. Superconductive to the nth degree. They're basically little bombs that could go off the minute somebody lights a damn match near a gel pack."

Askon's antennae drooped, but he didn't say anything.

"Except there's no sign anyone got off any shots near the engines," Warrick said. "Hell, like I said, the damn pipelines don't even have so much as a scratch on them." He ran a hand over his chin. "And somebody went through the trouble of pulling out all the gel packs and not a single stray shot hit them? There's frackin' piles of them. Not a scorch mark within two feet of any of them. Not one."

Askon's antennae straightened as he followed Warrick's theory. "You're suggesting the damage here was possibly self-inflicted?"

"Self-inflicted." Warrick grunted. "Sure. Let's call it that."

"You can't be certain of that."

Warrick pointed to the gel packs. "Those didn't end up there all by themselves. They didn't sprout legs and just walk out. And the damage in these consoles isn't natural decay over an extended period of time and it sure as hell isn't from any fusion blasts. These are all surface shots."

"This vessel is over five hundred years old," Askon pointed out.

"Sure. At some point five hundred years ago, somebody thought it would be a good idea to purposely depower this ship and then go out of their way to make sure that nobody was going to accidentally turn all the power back on."

Askon's antennae turned to face each other. "That's certainly a...theory, Commander."

"It's not a damn theory," Warrick said. "I've spent enough

time around space wrecks to know when it's a legitimate disaster or not. This," he twirled his finger around to indicate engineering, "has all the makings of being done on purpose."

Askon's antennae twitched uncomfortably. "I don't know that I can agree with your hypothesis."

"Fortunately then, I outrank you."

Askon paused and his antenna dipped forwards. "I don't think that's how that is supposed to work."

"Sure it is. Right, Nax?"

There was no response from Nax.

Warrick frowned and looked around, suddenly realizing that his friend wasn't anywhere in the immediate green glow. "Nax?"

Again there was no response.

Warrick turned to Askon. "Where the hell is he?"

"I have no idea," Askon replied.

"When was the last time you saw him?"

"Shortly after we entered engineering."

Warrick checked the time. "Shit. That was almost fifteen minutes ago." He looked suspiciously at Askon. "You haven't seen him or heard from him since?"

Askon didn't blink. "I'm afraid not, Commander and I would like to point out, before you go any further, neither have you."

Warrick muttered something under his breath. "Nax!" he shouted. There was no response. He double tapped his earpiece. "Warrick to Nax?"

There was no response over the communicator.

"Where the hell did he go?" Warrick asked. "Where the hell *could* he go?"

Warrick took a step towards the main engine coils, glancing around them. His flashlight didn't immediately illuminate anything of note in the darkness. He looked back at Askon. "Double back to the entrance. Maybe he fell down an open conduit."

Askon glanced nervously back at the darkness on the other side of the green glow.

Warrick fished out a few extra glow sticks and tossed them to Askon. "Here, make sure you don't fall down the same open conduit."

"Thank you," Askon replied, twisting the glow sticks and then disappeared back into the darkness.

"Nax, you orange bastard, you better be hurt," Warrick said, heading towards the section of engineering that was located on the other side of the coils.

The further Warrick got from the main engine coils, the shakier the floor panels became. Under the dim lighting of his flashlight he was able to make out more damage that looked suspect.

He paused near a fallen pylon. It was laying across the path, neatly bisecting what appeared to be a data core access panel in the opposite wall. Warrick looked around, trying to figure out where the pylon had fallen from. He spotted its original location about six feet above. It appeared to have been supporting a second deck or possibly a catwalk.

Warrick double-checked the angle of the pylon and then back up to where it was supposed to be. He shook his head. "How does it even make it down here like this? That's not bloody possible."

There was a noise to his left.

It was a soft noise, as though someone was coughing. But in the quiet stillness of the ship, it startled Warrick to the point he actually jumped a little.

He whipped his flashlight around to find Nax huddled off in a corner.

Warrick swore a Draeddur oath under his breath.

"Nax, you orange bastard, what the hell are you doing over there?"

Nax didn't respond.

Warrick frowned and stepped over the pylon, ducking a little so as to avoid the dangling wires.

"Nax?"

The helmsman didn't react to Warrick's voice. He stood in the small corner, his arms braced against the wall, almost as though it was attempting to close in on him.

"Nax, what the hell?" Warrick asked.

Natuzzi had no sweat glands. Nor did they have any tear ducts. In fact, they didn't excrete any bodily fluids beyond that of what they personally consumed.

And yet, if Warrick hadn't known this, he would have sworn his friend was sweating.

"Nax?"

Finally, Nax turned to face Warrick, as though just now noticing him.

His eyes were wide and his pupils were dilated. His arms were clearly trembling slightly as he pressed them against the wall.

Up close, Warrick was able to see that Nax's normally bright orange skin had taken on a duller, almost matte-like complexion. He was trying to remember the last time he had seen Nax like this, and he came up blank.

"Aw, brother," Warrick said, reaching for him. "What the hell is going on?"

Nax shook his head, pulling back from Warrick's outstretched hand. "No." His voice was unusually shaky.

"Nax-"

"Stay *back*," Nax snapped. Then he added, more softly, "Please forgive me. I...do not feel like myself."

"You don't much look like yourself, either," Warrick said. "In fact, you look like shit."

Nax winced. "Yes, that seems like an adequate description of my current state."

"Now I know something's wrong," Warrick said. "Last time I said you looked like shit you nearly clocked me one. What's going on?"

Nax took a deep breath and his whole body shuddered. "I'm...not certain." He spoke with an obvious effort, as though it pained him to utter every single word.

"Don't bullshit me right now, Nax," Warrick said. "We're in the middle of a saq'un space derelict and you look like you're about drop dead any second now."

Nax exhaled slowly and a tremor ran through his body. "I seem to be having some...difficulty."

"No. Shit," Warrick said.

Nax pulled his hands away from the wall, flexing his fingers in and out of a fist as they came to a rest at his side. "As I'm sure you recall, I, like all other Natuzzi, have an excellent sense of direction."

"Right. Sure. Your sense of universal harmony. You always know where you're located in the galaxy," Warrick said. "Great trick."

Nax winced. "As I've explained to you, it is not...a trick."

"I can rig up a nadion array and a linear databank discriminator that basically does the same thing," Warrick said. "It's a cool trick."

Nax winced again, but couldn't be bothered to muster up any real offense. "Since boarding this vessel, I have... lost that sense of direction."

"What the hell does that mean?" Warrick asked.

"I've been experiencing a...disorienting of some kind," Nax said. "I no longer have any true sense of direction. I feel...blind."

Warrick reached up to double tap his earpiece. "I'm calling the doc."

"*Wait.*"

"Nax, there's a reason Dheer's on the team."

"You don't understand."

"No kidding," Warrick said.

"That's not all." Nax took another unsteady breath. "I keep seeing *her*, Jaxson."

Warrick paused, arching an eyebrow. "Who?"

Nax swallowed, fighting to control the tremble in his arms. "*Grace.*"

18

THERE WAS nothing impressive about the door. In fact, if they hadn't been looking for it, they probably would have ignored the door altogether.

Keane rapped his knuckles against the door's dusty surface.

"Expecting someone to answer?" Dheer asked, pulling out her scanner.

"It would save us a lot of trouble," Keane replied.

The scanner didn't show anything new. It was the same data the ship's sensors had gathered. There were no other life signs on the other side of the door. "You're going to be disappointed."

Keane winced and rubbed his left hip.

"What's the matter?" Dheer asked, immediately moving closer to get some readings.

"I'm fine," Keane said, pushing her back. "It's just a little sore. I haven't walked this much lately."

"I told you, you shouldn't be here," Dheer said.

"I don't think we have to worry about me being out of

shape," Keane replied. "That's not the sort of thing that's going to get us all killed."

"Again, it's not the rest of us I'm worried about." Dheer moved her scanner closer to Keane's leg.

"Stop it." Keane moved out of her way, leaning against the wall for support.

"You're literally leaning against the wall so you don't fall over."

Keane took a step back and held up both hands away from the wall. "Better?"

Dheer just shook her head.

"As long as Warrick gets the main power up and running, I'll be fine," Keane said.

"How do you figure that?"

"Well, if he gets the main power back I don't have to hoof it all the way back to the shuttle," Keane said. "There's got to be at least one lift around here that'll get us in the general ballpark of the airlock."

"And if he doesn't get the power back?" Dheer asked, adjusting a setting on her scanner.

"Then I've suffered worse," Keane replied. "I won't like it, but I'm pretty sure I can handle the hike back."

Dheer frowned. "At least that's one of us."

"Commander, I think I've got something over here," Grell said.

Keane grabbed his cane from against the door and hobbled around Dheer.

"I can't believe the captain actually let you leave the ship in this condition," Dheer said.

The door was about six feet wide. Large enough to move several oversized cargo containers through it, if it was open. Grell stood on the far right side of the door, hunched over a panel emitting a soft white glow.

"Looks like Warrick was right," Grell said, pointing to the panel. "This room definitely has power."

Keane glanced at the panel and then around the darkened corridor that surrounded them. Outside of the dim lighting in the tunnel, this was the first sign of any power in the ship, besides the basic life support systems.

Keane turned back to the panel. There was a single, white icon visible. It was two half circles stacked back-to-back.

"Look familiar?" Keane asked.

Grell shook his head. "Can't say that it does."

Keane looked over his shoulder at Dheer. She shook her head, not even bothering to look up from her scanner.

"Alright. Well, we came all this way. Might as well see what happens," Keane said, reaching for the panel.

Dheer took two steps back.

"That inspires confidence," Keane said.

"You'll feel more inspired when you need me to keep you alive," Dheer replied.

Keane rolled his eyes and gently tapped the panel.

Immediately the icon disappeared and was replaced with a nine-panel input screen. Each panel contained a different combination of the two half circles.

"Okay, so it's a lock," Keane said.

"And how do you figure that?" Dheer asked.

He pointed to the door. "It didn't open and common sense says I'm gonna need to input a code on that."

Dheer studied the nine-panel grid. "Any ideas?"

Grell randomly tapped a few of the tabs in the grid. The panel flashed red and the door didn't open.

Dheer frowned and folded her arms. "Any other ideas?"

Grell shrugged. "It was worth a shot."

"Not really." Keane placed his cane against the wall

next to the panel. "I did a few years at the Earth embassy on Drosie." He pressed his fingers along the edge of the panel, looking for any separation. "The Bulrara monks there had a very interesting philosophy towards code-breaking."

"Codebreaking monks?" Dheer sounded dubious.

Keane found a seam along the bottom of the panel. Carefully, he pried it away from the wall, slipping his fingers between the panel's edge and the wall. After a few seconds the rest of the panel followed suit and popped off the wall.

"They weren't exactly codebreaking monks," Keane said. "But Spence Moretta and Gertie Price in Fleet Security found that their philosophies were strongly applicable to certain issues of security."

"Those names sound familiar," Grell said.

"They're two of the last surviving security experts of the Phaw Conflict in Twenty-Four-Seventy-Six," Kane said.

Now removed from the wall, the panel was only connected by a series of thick wires that disappeared into the wall.

Keane flipped the panel over so that he could still see the screen and the wires at the same time.

"It's all about finding the weakness," he continued. "For the Bulrara monks, that meant the weakness inside them. Like, a spiritual or emotional weakness. A character flaw. That sort of thing. Sounds easy, right? Well, they believed that your real weakness was hidden. That none of us truly understand what our weakness is. Personally, I thought it was all bullshit."

"That sounds about right," Dheer said.

"But Moretta and Price applied this philosophy to some basic codebreaking exercises and they found they were able to crack codes about thirty percent faster than using traditional methods." Keane ran his fingers along the length of the wires. "And then they applied it to a handful Phaw transmissions that we had never deciphered back during the Phaw Conflict of Seventy-Six. You know what happened?"

"They cracked the code," Dheer said with a distinct lack of surprise.

Keane looked at her and smiled. "They cracked the code. These transmissions were the bane of the Fleet Security for decades. We had broken every other code the Phaw had used, except for these. Experts had spent decades trying to figure it out and Moretta and Price did it in two days." Keane turned back to the panel and studied the grid for a moment. "Now, it's not an easy thing to comprehend, let alone master. Moretta and Price had been working with the monks for," he paused, thinking back on it. "I think it was almost a decade. They were practically honorary monks themselves by the end. Except, you know, they didn't go through with the castration part." Keane shook his head. "Anyway. While I was at the Embassy, I became friends with Moretta and Price. After they learned about my security background and interest in codebreaking, they took it upon themselves to try and teach me their techniques. They had done this a few times before with varied results. While it's a groundbreaking theory, it's extremely difficult to master and I was no exception. In fact, out of the forty people they taught, only three really mastered at their level. A few others picked up a handful of useful tricks and the rest just flunked out completely."

Keane gently yanked on two wires and the nine panel grid flashed and disappeared. Then he placed his index finger and thumb along the bottom edge of the panel and pressed it.

The nine panel grid reappeared for a second and then disappeared, leaving behind only six highlighted tabs. Keane quickly tapped each of the tabs in the order they were laid out.

The panel flashed green and the door opened with a soft hiss.

Keane grinned and grabbed his cane. "Obviously I wasn't one of the ones who flunked out completely."

"Obviously," Dheer said, checking her scanner to see if the readings were any different now that the door was open.

"I don't want you to think I'm some master codebreaker," Keane said. "Because I'm not."

"The thought never even crossed my mind," Dheer said, adjusting another setting on her scanner.

"I didn't really grasp the finer aspects of it," he continued. "However, I learned that it was really useful for picking locks."

"I'm sure your fourteen-year-old self would be really impressed," Dheer replied drily.

Keane nodded in agreement. "You know, he probably would. Most other, normal people would be impressed, too."

"Most other normal people haven't spent hours stitching you back together again," Dheer replied. "It puts things into perspective."

As they stepped into the room, the lights flickered on and suddenly, they knew where all the missing skulls had gone.

19

Mitchell found Steve waiting for him upon entering his quarters.

Steve greeted him with a massive, almost manic-like grin that faltered when Mitchell didn't seem to react at all. He took one look at Steve, still dressed in his admiral's uniform, and walked past him.

The smile dropped completely from Steve's face. "Well, that's not exactly the reaction I was expecting. If you don't mind me saying so, you don't seem surprised to see me."

Mitchell walked over to his liquor cabinet and poured himself a glass of a ninety-year-old scotch that Rabkin had left behind. "I had a hunch you'd be back."

"Oh, is that so?"

Mitchell studied his drink before taking a sip. "It's my experience that beings with god complexes don't know when to leave well enough alone."

Steve leveled Mitchell with a stern look. "It's not a complex."

Mitchell glanced back at him and shrugged. "Okay."

Steve didn't speak for a moment. "You're not an easy man to communicate with, Mitch."

"That's what my ex-wives say," Mitchell replied flatly.

Steve looked pointedly at the drink in Mitchell's hand. "Not going to offer me one? You're not a very good host."

"You're not a very good guest," Mitchell replied.

"True," Steve admitted. "But let's face it, at this point I can't actually just knock on your front door. It's not exactly *me*, if you know what I mean. And if I were to just appear outside your window and knock…Well, you may be made of sterner stuff than most men, Captain Mitchell, but I think that might give even you a genuine heart attack."

With one hand behind his back, Steve walked over to the bookcase on the far end of Mitchell's quarters, examining the titles with the intensity of an archeologist uncovering an ancient civilization. After a moment, he plucked a leather-bound book off the third shelf down from the top.

"Ooh, this is an interesting one." Steve flipped through the pages. He looked up at Mitchell, smirking. "I didn't take you for a romantic, Mitch."

"Be careful with that," Mitchell said, stepping behind his desk. "It's an original copy."

Steve flipped back to the copyright page. "So it is. Must have cost you a fortune."

"It was a gift."

"From an ex-wife?"

Mitchell looked at him suspiciously. "How do you know that?"

"Because you're not as much of a mystery as you think you are. Your entire life story is practically written across every cell in your body."

Mitchell didn't look convinced.

Steve sighed and placed the book back on the shelf. A second later, another, thicker, book appeared in his hand.

"This is how your concept of time appears to me. Large print. Easily referenced." He opened the book toward the end. "Want to know how it all ends? It's not as gory as you would think."

"I'll pass, thanks."

"Smart move." The book disappeared from Steve's hands. "Nothing good comes from knowing your future. I speak from personal experience, of course." He started pacing the length of the room.

Mitchell finished off his drink and set it down on his desk with a soft touch. "I thought you were done with us."

"I thought so, too," Steve agreed, wagging his finger. "Then I realized that perhaps I wasn't being fair to you."

"Did you come to this realization before or after you tortured my crewman?"

Steve nodded absently. "After, obviously. And torture? That's a bit...extreme, wouldn't you say? It was more of a sightseeing trip. Are you still sore about that?"

"Zemble's facing the possibility of permanent brain damage."

Steve rolled his eyes in an exaggerated fashion. "Oh, *please*. Don't be so *dramatic*. I told you, your little devil man will be *fine*."

"Not according to his doctor," Mitchell said.

"Oh, that little prehistoric medicine man?" Steve chuckled. "*Please*." He gave a dismissive wave as he glanced out the window at the ancient vessel that hung in space next to the *Defiance*. "That's like asking a caveman to examine a Natuzzi." He paused and then added flatly, "Oh, wait."

"You've been spying on us?" Mitchell said.

Steve made a face and shrugged awkwardly. "Spy-ing..." He snapped his fingers and the thick book reappeared in his hand. "I wouldn't call it spying if I already read the story."

"If you already know how it's going to end, then why the hell are you still here?"

"Because I like to view this particular book as a choose-your-own-adventure." The book disappeared again. "It's more interesting that way."

"To who?"

"Me, obviously." Steve shrugged. "I'm an omnipotent being. I need to do something to pass the eons."

"Is that what this is?" Mitchell asked. "You're just looking to kill time? You're bothering my crew because you're *bored*."

"I'm bothering your crew because I'm trying to keep them alive," Steve said. "I would have thought that you, of all people, would understand *that*."

"You don't have a very high opinion of us," Mitchell said.

"On the contrary, I actually think *very* highly of you," Steve said. "That's why I'm *here* in the first place."

"Could have fooled me."

Steve clapped his hands together. "Then somebody get me an Oscar because apparently I'm a master thespian!"

Mitchell wasn't amused.

Steve lowered his hands, clasping them behind his back. "You know, considering that I'm here to *help* you, you're being awfully *hostile* towards me."

"So far I haven't seen any examples of help."

Steve pursed his lips and squinted at Mitchell. "It occurs to me that we might have gotten off on the wrong foot."

"You know," Mitchell said, sitting down behind his desk. "I heard an interesting story earlier."

"Oh? Was it about a toga party that got out of hand?"

"Are you Zeus?" Mitchell asked.

For a split second Steve looked genuinely surprised. Then shook his head with a disappointed expression. "Do I look like the sort of being who goes around describing himself as a mad god?"

"A little bit."

"Then I'm really going to have to take some time to work on my personal presentation," he said. "Because I was going for 'benevolent god figure.'"

"Then you're definitely way off base," Mitchell said.

Steve folded his arms. "Apparently."

"Who was Zeus?"

"Does it matter?" Steve replied. "He's not here right now. In fact, I'm pretty sure he's still in a timeout. However, I am here and I'm here to tell you that you really need to get your people off that damn ship."

Mitchell glanced out at the *Eternal Hand of God*. "No." He sat down behind his desk.

Steve gaped at him. "No? *No?* Are you even *listening* to me?"

Mitchell just shrugged.

Steve just stared at him for a moment. "Are you really that dense, Captain? You and I both know that the Unity is on that vessel."

"I don't know that."

"Well *I* do," Steve said. "

"And our sensors don't confirm that."

"Of course they don't," Steve said. "Tell me, what do your sensors say about me?"

"You're not here."

"And yet I am."

"Are you?" Mitchell asked. "I seem to recall you questioning the nature of reality a moment ago."

Steve made a *tsk* noise. "Please, Captain, leave the

games to the professionals," he said. "You don't have the flair for it."

"If you've got something to say, say it and then get off my ship," Mitchell said. "I don't like stowaways."

"Stowaways." Steve shook his head. He clasped his hands behind his back and resumed pacing the length of the room. After a moment, he stopped and turned back to Mitchell. "Tell me, Captain Gavin Mitchell, what do you know about the Unity?"

Mitchell didn't answer right away. He tapped his fingers against the surface of his desk, watching the strange man pacing his quarters, trying to get a read on him.

"They're a culture from another dimension here to assimilate us," Mitchell said after a moment.

"And?"

"They haven't been very successful."

"*Yet.*"

"Excuse me?"

"They haven't been very successful *yet*," Steve said. "It's only a matter of time and time is something the Unity has plenty of. And in time, as always, the Unity is always successful."

"I think you've been skipping a few sections in your book," Mitchell said. "We already discovered the Unity can't survive in our dimension."

Steve just stared at Mitchell in mild disbelief for a moment.

"They. Can't. Survive." Steve chuckled.

Mitchell frowned. "What's the joke?"

"The joke?" Steve took a deep breath and then exhaled slowly. "It's that you people truly are as simple-minded as they say. Tell me, Captain Mitchell, are you familiar with the cockroach?"

Mitchel's brow furrowed in confusion and irritation "The cockroach?"

Steve nodded. "An Earth insect. Vile, gross, creepy little thing. They have them on Chorix, too and, if you can believe it, they're still not as disgusting as the Earth variety. They can survive practically anything, yes? Even a nuclear holocaust."

Mitchell exhaled impatiently. "I know what a damn cockroach is."

"Well," Steve pressed his hands together. "That's what the Unity is, Mitch. An interdimensional, cosmic cockroach. It can and *will* survive in *any* environment.

"Do you have any proof to back this up?"

"*Proof?* I'm a god-like being standing before you and you're asking for *proof* of what I'm saying?"

"If you're about to make some half-assed speech about faith, save it," Mitchell said.

"I would never presume to lecture a representative of the human race on *faith*," Steve said, dripping with sarcasm. "What I will do is give you a crash course on the nature of reality."

"This should be interesting."

"Oh, I can guarantee that you're going to learn something that will most definitely blow your mind. You see, reality is a *stack*. Different dimensions, alternate realities, they're stacked atop each other, endlessly so in both directions. Up and down. Except, there is a *bottom* and there is a *top*." He held up his left hand. "At the absolute very top are my people." Under his left hand he placed his right hand. "And at the very, very, *very* bottom of reality, beneath literally every other dimension in existence, down in the eternal darkness where there not only is no light, but the very *hint* of light is an alien concept. Down here is where the Unity is from."

Steve gestured to the ship outside Mitchell's windows. "That vessel out there? It's not from this reality. It's not even from a reality nearby. It's from one of the dimensions that have already been consumed by the dark well of the Unity."

Mitchell sat back in his seat and held out his hands. "Any proof to back this up?"

Steve smacked his hands across his face. "Proof? *Proof?* Egads, man! What is this obsession with *proof?* This is not a court of *law. Proof? Proof?* Your people have already found evidence of the Unity on that ship."

"My people found a Fleet badge that used to belong to a man who a died a hundred years ago during our first encounter with the Unity," Mitchell said. "It's a curious mystery. Hardly damning evidence of a pending attack."

Steve jabbed his finger violently at him. "You have had *personal* encounters with the Unity. You know, on some level, everything I'm saying is *true.*"

"I also know that I don't know you from a stray asteroid," Mitchell said. "For all I know, you're connected to that ship out there. For all I know, you're the real threat here and this is some elaborate trap that *you've* concocted."

Steve straightened, looking down upon Mitchell. "I don't need *traps.* I don't need *schemes.*"

He snapped his fingers and instantly Mitchell's quarters erupted into massive, burning flames.

Before Mitchell could react, Steve snapped his fingers again and the flames disappeared. Mitchell's quarters were restored completely, without any hint of the fire.

Mitchell struggled to maintain his composure. He fought the urge to check himself for any signs of burns or injuries, despite not feeling any different than he had a moment ago.

Steve stepped up to Mitchell's desk and pressed the

palms of his hands against the surface as he leaned forward. "Listen to me very carefully, Captain Gavin Mitchell, you *need* to get your people off that ship. The longer you leave them there, the less likely any of them come home *alive*."

Standing this close to him, Mitchell became aware of the fact that Steve had no odor. He didn't smell. There was no scent at all.

There was a double chirp from Mitchell's comm.

He twisted in his seat and tapped the small panel on the corner of his desk. "Go for Mitchell."

"You might want to get back down to sickbay," Rabkin said. "Zemble's awake."

Mitchell looked up to see Steve's reaction, but Steve was already gone.

20

"DOCTOR RABKIN SAID I was only gone for a few minutes." Zemble paused, his bloodshot eyes staring off at something that couldn't be seen by anyone else. "Didn't feel like that."

Zemble sat on the edge of his exam table, his fingers gripping the underside of the table so tightly that he was causing minor indentations. Color was slowly returning to his skin but it was his eyes that concerned Mitchell. They were distant and dazed, with a cloudy vagueness that Mitchell had never seen in his security officer before.

Mitchell glanced at Rabkin. The old man stood at the foot of the exam table, almost off to the side, his arms folded. He raised his bushy eyebrows as if to say, 'Don't look at me, I thought he was going to be brain dead.'

Mitchell turned back to Zemble. "Where were you, Lieutenant?"

Zemble didn't answer right away. He just stared off into some unseen distance. After a few moments, Mitchell was beginning to think he hadn't heard him. He started to ask again when Zemble blinked and, for the first time since arriving in sickbay, he looked directly at Mitchell.

"I...honestly don't know, Captain." Zemble's voice was scratchy, almost hoarse, as though he spent hours screaming. "It felt...familiar but different. I was..." He trailed off for a moment, the distant look returning to his eyes. Zemble blinked again and refocused on Mitchell. "I was alone, but surrounded."

"Surrounded by what?" Mitchell asked.

Zemble's eyes widened slowly and he shook his head. "Nothing."

Mitchell frowned. "You're not giving me much here, Mr. Zemble."

"I'm sorry, Captain. I wish I could be more helpful, but..." Zemble trailed off again. His gaze drifted from Mitchell to a blank monitor just over the captain's shoulder. Zemble tilted his head slightly and asked, "I was only gone for a few minutes?"

"Not even," Mitchell said. "Two minutes and fourteen seconds."

Zemble blinked and focused once again on Mitchell. "Really? It felt like months."

"Months?" Mitchell echoed.

"Maybe even years," Zemble said. "Could have only been days, I suppose. But minutes?" He shook his head slowly. "No, that's not possible." Zemble rubbed his eyes and looked at Mitchell apologetically. "I'm sorry, Captain. I know that doesn't make sense. I just...I wish I could be more helpful."

"Don't be sorry." Mitchell placed a hand on Zemble's shoulder. "I'm just glad to have you back." He turned to Rabkin and gestured for the old man to follow him to the other side of sickbay where they would be out of earshot. "Well?

The old man shrugged. "Don't look at me. Half hour

ago I was pretty sure he was going to be a vegetable for the rest of his natural life, which wasn't going to be very long."

"You have to have some idea," Mitchell said.

Rabkin glanced back at Zemble who was now talking with the nurse. "I really don't. He just woke up a few minutes before I called you."

"Any brain damage?"

"None that we can see. I want to run a few more tests, but he's cleared all the basics. He knows who he is, who I am, where we are, what year it is and who the vice president is. And that last one is pretty damn amazing, because even I don't know who that bastard is. I had to double check his answer against the computer." Rabkin exhaled. "I'd like to keep him around for a few days for observation, but so far he seems to be in perfect health. Don't ask me how, though. I compared his current readings to the ones we took a half hour ago and it's like night and day. There's no indication he suffered any oxygen deprivation. Hell, if I didn't know any better, I'd say he just took some really bad Vorth mushrooms."

Mitchell rubbed his chin. "What happened when he woke up?"

"You wondering if he jolted awake screaming about something in some weird language that could provide a clue as to where he had gone?" Rabkin asked.

"Not in so many words," Mitchell said. "But yeah."

Rabkin grunted. "No such luck. Our boy just woke up like he had been taking a nap. First thing out of his mouth was what was he doing in sickbay."

"Did he seem confused?"

"Sure," Rabkin said. "But it was the kind of confused that you might get when you go to sleep in one place and wake up in another."

"Doctor?" A nurse quietly interrupted them, handing Rabkin a datapad.

Rabkin frowned as he skimmed through the information on the pad.

"What is it?" Mitchell asked.

"Zemble's blood work," Rabkin said. "What do you know about Elwat blood?"

Mitchell thought about it for a second, then slowly shook his head. "Just some vague memories from Xenobiology One-oh-One back at the Academy. And it's blue."

"Average human has nine to twelve pints of blood," Rabkin said.

"Sure," Mitchell said. "That one I know. But you asked me about Elwats."

"Let me finish before you start with the smartass routine," Rabkin grumbled.

"Okay, but it's not as fun that way," Mitchell said.

"Your average Elwat has almost three times as much blood running through them," Rabkin continued. "In case you hadn't noticed, they're a bit bigger than us."

"It's been pointed out to me once or twice."

Rabkin held up the data so Mitchell could see the results. "Zemble's platelet level is way below average for an Elwat his age and size. In addition, his blood is so thinned out right now, you give him a basic paper cut and he'll probably bleed to death."

"What does that mean?"

Rabkin looked over the results again and shrugged. "Hell if I know. The only time I've seen these kinds of results on an Elwat before, they were battling stage four inflammatory skin cancer. Zemble tested negative for that."

Mitchell sighed, rubbing a hand over his chin.

"I know this looks bad, but it's nothing he won't

recover from in a day or two," Rabkin said. "Weird as hell, but I don't think he's going to drop dead from it."

Mitchell folded his arms. "I had a visitor in my quarters."

One of Rabkin's bushy eyebrows went up. "Oh? I'm guessing you didn't learn your lesson from the last time you got involved with a subordinate."

Mitchell glared at him. "It was Steve."

Rabkin frowned. "Well, shit."

"Yeah."

"Can't say I'm surprised, though," Rabkin said. "He had that pain-in-the-butt air about him. What'd he want this time?"

"Same thing as before," Mitchell said. "He wanted me to pull the away team off that ship."

"Insistent little bastard. He give a reason why this time?"

Mitchell hesitated before answering. He glanced around to make sure no one was listening in. "Apparently he seems to think the Unity's onboard."

"Shit," Rabkin muttered.

"Yeah," Mitchell agreed.

"That's a hell of a thing to say."

"Don't I know it."

"What do you think?"

Mitchell shrugged. "After what happened on Carlock and based on all the data we pulled from the Veneer base there, the Unity shouldn't be a problem."

"But?"

"But I don't want to be the guy who's going around looking for an alien threat in every dark corner," Mitchell said.

"That's not what I meant," Rabkin said.

"I know." Mitchell sighed. "I had Sadler run another

sensor sweep of the ship, checking it against the data we pulled from the Veneer base."

"And?"

Mitchell shook his head. "Not a damn thing."

"So there's no Unity onboard."

"That's what the sensors say."

"You don't sound convinced."

"My faith in the way the nature of reality is supposed to work has been shaken a little bit today," Mitchell admitted.

"Fair enough," Rabkin said.

"Something's not adding up here." He looked at Zemble. "What's the connection between that ship, this Steve being and the Unity?"

"Maybe there isn't one."

"Maybe."

"Maybe somebody's just trying to screw with us," Rabkin said.

Mitchell nodded. "Maybe."

The main doors to sickbay opened and Calloway stepped in, clearly heading for Zemble. However, the moment she noticed Mitchell and Rabkin off to the side, she stopped abruptly in the open doorway.

She stared at Mitchell and Rabkin and then took an awkward half a step back. When the doors started to close she abruptly took a step forward again, but didn't move past the doorway, keeping the doors open.

"You're either in or you're out," Rabin said. "My open door policy doesn't extend to literally keeping the doors to sickbay open so every Tom, Dick and Harry can gawk at my patients when they pass by."

"Right," Calloway squeaked and took a step back out into the hallway.

The doors slid shut.

Rabkin and Mitchell looked at each other, but before they could say anything the doors slid open again.

This time Calloway stepped all the inside.

As the doors closed behind her she said, "I think I meant to be on this side. Sorry."

Rabkin raised a bushy eyebrow. "You think?"

"I know?" she said hesitantly.

"Ensign, I don't want you to take this the wrong way, but are you here to steal some opiates?" Rabkin asked.

Calloway's mouth flapped open and closed, but nothing came out.

Mitchell shot him a look.

"Oh, bite me," Rabkin grumbled. "It's my sickbay and I'll be as much of an asshole as I feel like." He disappeared into his office before Mitchell could reply.

Calloway made a bizarre effort of looking everywhere except at her captain.

"Ms. Calloway, is there a problem?" Mitchell asked.

"Well, technically, I am supposed to be on the bridge right now," she admitted.

Mitchell wordlessly raised an eyebrow.

"But, Commander Sadler said it was okay," Calloway said in a voice that was closer to a whisper than not.

"What was?"

"To come down here and see Zemble," Calloway said. "I heard he was awake."

Mitchell gestured at the large red Elwat who was clearly very much awake and watching their conversation.

"Yes. Right, Okay." Calloway bobbed her head, but didn't move. "Is it, um, okay for me to be here right now?"

"As I understand it, Mr. Zemble's not under any quarantine," Mitchell said.

"Right, sure," Calloway said. She started to move forward again and then stopped. "It's just that I didn't think you were going to be down here. Not that I didn't think you shouldn't be down here or that I was trying to come down here in secret or that I'm trying to avoid you because I'm not trying to do any of those things or thinking any of those things. I guess, I actually meant, like, um, well…I'm not going to get in trouble for, like, abandoning my station, am I?"

Mitchell looked at her, bemused. "It's not abandoning your station if you were given permission."

Calloway bobbed her head again. "Right. Sure. Sure. That makes sense. A lot of sense, really. Sorry. Sir." She cleared her throat awkwardly.

"Ensign?"

"Yes, Captain? Sir?" Calloway swallowed nervously.

"I understand the circumstances are what they are right now, but you really need to *relax*," Mitchell said. "Consider it an order."

Calloway bobbed her head. "Yes, sir."

Mitchell nodded at Zemble. "Say hi to your friend." He turned and stepped into Rabkin's office. "I don't think I've ever met anyone more high-strung than that young lady."

Rabkin didn't respond, he just stood there, his back to Mitchell.

Frowning, Mitchell took a step around him and started to say something else.

But the words never made it out of his mouth once he saw Steve sitting there behind Rabkin's desk.

21

"THERE MUST BE HUNDREDS," Keane said, eyeing the skulls as they slowly walked through the room.

"Thousands," Dheer corrected him, occasionally glancing down at her scanner. "Hundreds of different species, though."

"That's not making me feel any better," Keane said, his hand resting on the handle of the fusion pistol.

They spoke quietly, as though almost afraid of what might happen if they were too loud in this room of skulls.

The skulls were neatly stacked atop one another, stretching from the floor to the ceiling. Each one was perfectly preserved. They filled the room, but left a clear path just wide enough for the three members of the away team to walk single file.

Beams of light illuminated the room from under the floor, casting the light out up through the skulls.

Grell took the lead, slowly taking them through the short winding path and doing his best not to stare at any one skull for too long.

Dheer, however, couldn't take her eyes off the skulls.

There was something about them that bothered her beyond their macabre display.

She adjusted the settings on her scanner.

There was nothing particularly unique about the way the skulls were preserved. But there was something in the readings on her scanner that troubled her.

"What's the point of this?" Keane asked. "What does somebody get out of taking all these skulls and stacking them away like this? I don't understand it."

"The natives on Phixelara believe the soul resides in the physical heart," Grell said. "When one of them passes away they remove the heart and burn it so that the soul of the deceased can be freed to join the afterlife."

Keane gave him a sideways look. "How is that something you know?"

Grell shrugged. "I suffer from insomnia. I read a lot when I can't sleep."

"Hang on," Dheer said, stopping in front of a selection of human skulls. Her attention was still focused on her scanner, double checking the readings.

Keane paused and looked back at her. "What's the matter?"

Dheer glanced up at him. "You mean other than an entire room filled with thousands of skulls?"

Keane rolled his eyes. "Yes, other than that."

She held up her scanner. "Something's not right."

"That's a hell of an understatement," Grell muttered. He quietly moved on, disappearing around a corner.

"Here." Dheer handed her scanner to Keane and then carefully attempted to extract one of the skulls from the stack.

Keane eyed the stack uncomfortably. "Are you sure that's a good idea? The last thing I need right now is to be buried alive here."

"Hush," Dheer whispered at him. She slowly worked the skull out from its spot. The rest of the row swayed slightly.

When none of the other skulls dropped on them, Keane exhaled, unaware that he had been holding his breath.

Once she had the skull removed, Dheer held it up for a closer look.

There was a vague, almost yellowish coating over the skull's surface, giving it a smooth and polished feel, almost as though it was covered in wax.

"No, that's not it," she muttered. "Where is it?"

"Where's what?" Keane asked.

Dheer didn't bother to answer him.

As Dheer examined the skull, Keane glanced at the screen on her scanner and immediately saw what confusing her.

"That can't be right," he said.

"Here." Dheer turned the skull over so that they could see the inside of it.

The interior of the skull was lined with a series of marks that the scanner immediately recognized as data strips. According to the scanner, there was almost sixteen zettabytes of data stored within the skull.

Keane shook his head, looking back and forth between the skull and the scanner. "No way."

Dheer put the skull back and pulled out another one. This one she recognized as having formerly belonged to an Aurrod. Again, on the interior of the skull, there were a dozen data strips that wrapped around it. It contained almost twice as much data as the human skull had.

Keane rubbed a hand across his chin as he looked around the room full of skulls and then back at the scanner. "Each one of these?"

"That's what it looks like," Dheer said.

"That could be…" he trailed off for a moment, trying to do some quick calculations in his head. "No, that's not possible. We're looking at possibly the largest data repository ever." He shook his head. "No, not possible."

Dheer gestured with her hand at the skulls. "And yet…"

"Who stores that much data on the inside of a skull?" Keane asked.

"Are you aware of how much information the brain contains over an individual's lifespan?" Dheer asked.

"That's not what I'm asking," Keane said. "You know what I mean."

"Sure." She put the skull back carefully and selected another human one to examine.

"The brain is one thing," Keane continued. "Someone or someones went out of their way to store data on the inside of these skulls *after* these people passed away. Nobody in the entire galaxy does that. Not only is it not practical, but it would violate all sorts of laws. Half the planets in Alliance have something on the books about not desecrating the dead and the UPA itself draws a pretty hard line in the sand over it."

Dheer took her scanner back. "This is hardly desecrating the dead."

"Someone removed thousands of skulls from thousands of dead bodies and then found a way to store at least sixteen zettabytes of data in each skull," Keane said. "What would you call it?"

Dheer adjusted a setting on her scanner. "An act of desperation."

"An act of desperation?" Keane gaped at her. "How?"

"Because it's a lot of work for it to be anything else,"

Dheer said, she angled the scanner to get a visual of the data strips inside the skull.

Keane didn't know what to say to that. He ran a hand through his hair, just staring at the rows of skulls.

"Here we go. I think I've got something," Dheer said. She moved next to Keane so he could see the screen with her. "They're dot-based data strips, right? Each dot contains a certain amount of data."

"Sure."

"Well, look at this," Dheer said, scrolling through the information the scanner was downloading from the data strip. "Millions of pages, photos and videos in this skull alone."

"This is not a practical method of data storage," Keane said. "What happens if any of these skulls are damaged?"

"What happens when a hard drive gets damaged?" Dheer countered.

"I don't-" Keane looked at her, confused. "You think this is a good idea? How are you not bothered by this?"

"There's an entire segment of the Phaw culture that's essentially built around assisted suicide," Dheer said as she skimmed through the documents. "It doesn't matter whether you're old, young, sick or healthy. If you want to end your life, there's a system in place for that. It's not illegal. It's not even frowned upon."

"In the UPA it is," Keane said.

"And the Phaw aren't members of the UPA," Dheer replied. "And even if they were," she looked at him. "Their culture is their culture. It's not my business to tell them how to live, or end, their lives." She turned back to the scanner. "Just because we think it's weird, creepy or wrong, doesn't mean that it's not a sacred tradition with another species."

"That's a human skull in your hand," Keane pointed out.

"Yes it is," Dheer agreed. "But I think it's safe to say that wherever this ship is from, it's not from around here."

"Commander, Doctor," Grell called from up ahead. "You're gonna want to see this."

Dheer and Keane made their way down the narrow path towards Grell.

The path abruptly opened up into a wide circular space. At the center of the space, surrounded by a thick magnetic field and three consoles, was a silver ball hovering in midair.

"What is it?" Keane asked.

"I have no idea," Grell replied. "The magnetic field is blocking the scanner."

Keane walked around and looked over Grell's shoulder at his scanner. "That field's almost as strong as the *Defiance's* main deflectors. How did our sensors not pick that up?"

"You got me," Grell said.

Keane examined one of the consoles. "This is where the distress call is being transmitted from."

"This doesn't make sense," Dheer said. She set the skull down on a console and looked at Grell and Keane. "The data here is basically mundane stuff. It's like someone's life story and it doesn't look very interesting."

Keane looked around at the skulls surrounding them. "You think that's in all of these? Some kind of, I don't know, memorial?"

"Okay, sure," Dheer said. "Why not? But what's the point of it? And who's it a memorial for?"

"Hang on," Grell said, working the third console. "I think I've got something here."

A three-dimensional hologram appeared off to the left of them. It was an image of an Asian man in his late fifties, dressed in a uniform that was similar to theirs. Only where theirs was black and gray, his uniform was black and white. The badge on his left breast was immediately recognizable as a Fleet badge with the rank of captain.

The holographic imaged flickered for a moment as if it was going to disappear. Then it stabilized and the man began to speak.

The language the man was using was unfamiliar to the away team. There were a handful of words here and there that sounded similar to words they had heard before, but nothing sounded quite right.

As he continued to speak, the program cycled its way through a few more languages, each one more familiar to the away team.

Then the hologram paused.

"What happened?" Keane asked.

Grell looked down at the console. "I have no idea. I didn't touch anything."

The hologram flickered as it reset back to its starting point and the man began to speak, this time in perfect English.

"My name is Captain Wu Xuefeng. This ship is all that is left not only of my world, but my universe."

22

"HERE'S THE *THING*, MITCH," Steve said, kicking his feet up on Rabkin's desk. "You don't strike me as a stupid man. Perhaps you're not the most intelligent individual your species has to offer, but that doesn't necessarily mean you're *stupid*. You see, I tend to be an excellent judge of character and I judge your character to be, well, fairish. I mean, after all, I am judging you against the character of literally everyone else in this reality. So, really, you should feel flattered by that assessment."

"Jim?" Mitchell moved in front of Rabkin and put his hands on both of the old man's shoulders. "Jim?" Rabkin stared off into the distance, unresponsive. He didn't budge as Mitchell shook his shoulders. Mitchell turned to Steve. "What the hell did you do to him?"

Steve frowned. "Are you even listening to me? I'm trying to pay you a compliment. Well, I suppose, it's a rather backhanded compliment when you think about it. Because it's still a poor commentary on the fact you let that *woman-thing* walk around your ship unsupervised."

Mitchell slammed his fists into Rabkin's desk and Steve actually jumped a little, his feet sliding off.

"You listen to me, you little cosmic *shithole*," Mitchell snapped. "I don't know who the hell you or what the hell you are, but if you don't stop attacking my people I will make it my life's mission to hunt you down and find a way to put you out of our galaxy's misery."

Steve didn't say anything for a moment, he just stared at Mitchell.

And then he broke out into a grin.

"That was pretty good," Steve said. He rolled up his sleeve and showed Mitchell his arm. "I almost had goosebumps here." He leaned forward across the desk. "You know what I like about you, Mitch? You've got *balls*. Big, brass balls. There aren't a lot of beings in the multiverse who'd have the balls to talk to me like that. Well done."

Steve raised his hand and snapped his fingers.

Rabkin's body suddenly slouched forward, as though it had been released from an invisible grip.

"What the hell?" Rabkin grumbled, holding a hand to his forehead.

Mitchell spun around to face him. "Jim, are you okay?"

"What the hell kind of question is that?" Rabkin said. "You a doctor all of a sudden? If I tell you I'm not, what the hell are you going to do about it?" He pushed Mitchell out of his way and pointed at Steve. "And what the hell are you doing in my seat?"

"Keeping it warm." Steve bounced to his feet in one fluid motion.

Rabkin looked at Mitchell. "What the hell is going on here?"

Steve clasped his hands behind his back as he made his way around the desk. "You know, you should be grateful. I could have sent your old witch doctor to the same place I sent your devil man. Instead I simply froze him." He held out his hands. "If that doesn't say benevolent benefactor… Well, I really don't know what does."

Rabkin grunted. "If you're a benevolent benefactor, then I'm a damn one-eyed space pirate."

Steve shot him a look. "*You* especially should be more grateful. You wouldn't last five seconds where I sent the devil man."

"And care to tell us where that was?" Rabkin asked, unfazed.

Steve waved a hand in an ethereal manner. "How does one describe a sunset to a man born blind?"

"You fancy yourself a real poetic asshole, don't you?" Rabkin said.

Steve grinned at him. "As a matter of fact, I do."

"What the hell are you doing here?" Mitchell asked.

"The same thing I've been trying to do ever since I got here," Steve said. "Impart a little bit of my infinite wisdom and maybe save a few of your sorry souls in the process. You know, I can't help but notice that your people are still on that deathtrap."

"They're investigating its origins," Mitchell said.

"I can tell you where it came from," Steve said. "It came from a lower reality that was consumed by the Unity. That ship out there is all that's left of an *entire reality*. Happy now? Any other mysteries I can clear up for you while you get your people off there? Perhaps you're still wondering about how many angels you can get to dance on the point of a needle? Well, the answer's forty-two. But the real problem is finding that many angels who want to dance."

"What the hell is he talking about?" Rabkin asked Mitchell.

Steve clapped his hands. "Oh, this is *perfect*. I'd love to see how you break this down for him. It'll be interesting to see if you've been paying attention to me."

"Apparently, according to our friend here," Mitchell said. "Reality is apparently a stack."

"The hell is that supposed to mean?" Rabkin grumbled.

Steve nodded. "Yes, yes. A visual aid is clearly in order."

He pressed his hands together, on top of each other and then spread them out. As he did so, a hazy image of a wide cylinder appeared, cut into dozens of slices.

Steve paused and glanced up at them. "Obviously this should go without saying, but this isn't to scale."

He turned back to the growing cylinder between his hands.

The top of the cylinder turned bright white.

The bottom was black.

Tendrils of darkness slowly spread up from the bottom, consuming the other slices as they went.

Steve pulled his hands away and took a step back, leaving the cylinder floating there.

"*This* is how reality works," Steve said. He pointed to the darkness that was slowly making its way up the cylinder. "*This* is the Unity, working its way through the stacks of reality, consuming every little universe, reality and dimension as it goes."

The tendrils kept growing, moving farther up. They spread out so that there were multiple points of contact in each slice of the cylinder, as though they were anchoring themselves in order to pull the rest of the darkness up with them.

"This is where you are," Steve pointed to a slice somewhere in the middle where only the tips of a few of the dark tendrils had pierced. "This is where I'm from." He gestured to the pure, untouched white at the top. "It's a beautiful paradise. I could tell you more about it, but I'm afraid any apt description would quite literally blast your feeble little minds apart."

"You don't have a lot of friends, do you?" Rabkin asked.

"And this," Steve pointed to the slice of the stack that was completely consumed by the darkness, "is where that ship out there is from. Note how the Unity has completely consumed it. Note the all-consuming darkness. Note there's literally nothing left except for a dead ship that's slowly making its way up through the stacks in a vain attempt to warn other realities about the coming threat." Steve laughed. "Like *that's* going to do any good."

"It could," Mitchell said. "You never know how some information may be beneficial to certain places."

Steve nodded. "Yes, yes. Of course. Tell me something, Mitch." He pointed to the floating cylinder of reality. "Do you happen to notice a slice there between your reality and where the *Eternal Hand of God* came from? Perhaps a slice that seems completely and utterly devoid of the Unity? Because I don't."

"And we're just supposed to just trust you blindly?" Rabkin asked. "Like you're some kind of expert on the Unity? We don't know who the hell you are. For all we know, you're working with the Unity."

Steve pointed his finger at Rabkin. "That's a stupid thing to say and I'm just going to ignore it because, quite frankly, talking to you is like talking to a rusty wheel that's long outlived its usefulness and could fall apart at any moment." He turned to Mitchell. "You, however, Captain, I find to be a little more open-minded." He paused. "Am I mixing my metaphors?" Steve shook his head. "Never mind. Are you getting the picture yet, Captain?"

Mitchell studied the cylinder for a moment and then looked up at Steve. "I'm getting a picture. But so far it's of an annoying entity who seems unusually desperate to convince me that my ship's in danger."

"And you seem very intent on ignoring my warnings," Steve said. "I'm seriously considering reevaluating my assessment of your character, *Mitch*." He pointed in the direction of where the *Eternal Hand of God* was located just off their bow. "That ship out there is all that's left an entire reality that's been consumed by the Unity. Do you really think it made its way all the way here without bringing something with it? Nothing escapes the Unity unscathed," he said. "Or haven't you figured that out yet?"

Calloway's laughter pierced the momentary silence and the expression on Mitchell's face changed.

Steve wagged a finger at him. "Here that, gentlemen? That's the sound of the bells going off."

Rabkin looked back and forth between Mitchell and Steve. "What the hell is he talking about?"

"Ensign Calloway," Mitchell said.

"That's adorable," Steve said. "It has a *name*. It's a disaster on two feet that could kill all of you at any moment and it has the cutest little name. *Adorable*."

"What do you know about Calloway?" Rabkin asked.

"A hell of a lot more than you do, medicine man," Steve said. "How long have you been looking her over? The answer's practically been in your face this entire time. Really, it's amazing that anyone trusts you to even fix their damn paper cuts."

Rabkin bunched his hands into fists. "Buddy, I don't know what the hell you are, but I know that if you don't change your tone real soon, I know what you're gonna be."

"Oh, that's hilarious," Steve said flatly. "You're going to pick a fistfight with me? And people think you're *smart*."

"Answer his question," Mitchell said. "What do you know about Erin Calloway?"

Steve stared at Rabkin for a moment longer, as if daring him to come around the desk at him. Then he turned to Mitchell. "I know that she's a time bomb waiting to go off at literally any second," Steve said. "And you idiots have given her free reign of your ship. You should have shoved her out the nearest airlock the minute you discovered what she was."

"The problem is, we don't know what she is," Mitchell said.

Steve barked out a laugh. "Oh, that is *rich*." He shook his head. "That is..." He trailed off, chuckling to himself.

"Alright, smartass," Rabkin grumbled. "What the hell is she?"

The amusement dropped from Steve's face abruptly. "She's Unity, that's what she is. And if you didn't realize that before this very moment, then you're both bigger fools than I took you for."

"Ensign Calloway is not a member of the Unity," Mitchell said.

"Of course she isn't," Steve said. "One doesn't become a *member* of the Unity. It's not a *club*. They don't have dues or a president or a treasury officer. It's a *disease*. You become *infected* by the Unity. It *consumes* you. I shouldn't have to be explaining this to you. This is the basic nature of the threat you're facing, if you don't already know this, then what the hell am I even doing here?"

"Except that before Carlock, Ensign Calloway never had any encounter with the Unity," Rabkin said. "She was Earthbound her entire life until she was assigned to the *Defiance*."

"Oh my goodness." Steve made a face. "Do I have to *spell* it out for you? Do you want me to take the marker and connect all the little dots for you? Should I hold your hand whilst I do it? Maybe I can explain it all using two-syllable words. Would that work for you?" He snapped his fingers in both of their faces. "*Listen to me.* I shouldn't have to tell you this. You should have figured it out on your own already. The Unity has already *infected Earth*."

23

"Go sit down," Warrick said.

"I'm *fine*," Nax said, not moving from his spot behind Warrick.

"Ten minutes ago you were a Scorkrin piss puddle," Warrick said. "And now you're fine? Sit. Down."

Nax looked at him coolly. "Need I remind you that while you do, technically, outrank me, I am still the leader of this away team."

"You don't need to remind me of anything." Warrick walked around him and gathered up a handful of the gel packs that still had plenty of the deep green color left in them. "Unless you want to remind me why I bother listening to you." Warrick circled around the main engine coils to the side opposite Nax.

Nax took a moment to compose himself. He glanced back at Askon, but the Knok's attention was focused on his own repair work. Nax made his way around to Warrick's side of the main engines.

Warrick popped open six slots on the main engine coils that were perfectly sized to hold the gel packs. He reached in and pulled out a handful of wires that seemed frayed at the ends.

"Jaxson," Nax began.

"What the hell do you think you're doing out here?" Warrick said, stripping the wires.

"If you're speaking to the issue of my current state," Nax said. "I would have to point out that I didn't know this was going to happen. Clearly, had I known, I would not have accepted this assignment."

Warrick stopped working on the wires and looked back at Nax. "Seriously?"

Nax looked confused. "Why would you think I'm not being serious?"

Warrick sighed and knocked his forehead against the engine coils. "Nax, damnit. I'm talking about *Grace*."

Nax winced at the mention of her name. "Yes. Obviously, my condition has some kind of hallucinatory side effect."

"You *think*?"

"Obviously I don't dispute it as I am the one who mentioned it to you."

"And you don't think this has anything to do with your lack of sleeping lately?" Warrick asked him. He grabbed one of the gel packs and carefully inserted it into the slot, connecting the wires he had stripped into their appropriate spots on the gel pack.

Nax didn't respond right away.

Warrick finished up with the second gel pack before turning back to him. "Seriously?"

"I don't know that I feel comfortable drawing a connection from one condition to the other," Nax said carefully. "Also, there didn't appear to be any potential side effects to my lack of sleep prior to this mission."

Warrick pointed his photon wrench at him. "That's bullshit and you know it."

Nax tilted his head to the side. "I would disagree."

"Of course you would." Warrick grabbed the three remaining gel packs and slid them into their respective slots. "Because that's the kind of bullshit artist you are."

"Doctor Rabkin would also disagree."

"And I'm sure you passed along all sorts of relevant medical data on the Natuzzi that could help the old man properly diagnose you," Warrick said.

Nax didn't respond to that either.

"That's what I thought."

"Jaxson," Nax tried again.

Warrick cut him off immediately. "Your people have a problem with hallucinations."

"That's a fairly broad and potentially inflammatory statement," Nax said.

"It's also the damn truth, Nax," Warrick said. "I spent six years on your planet. You know how many Natuzzi I ran into suffering from Fey's Euphoria?"

"This is not Fey's," Nax said firmly.

"You just told me you're seeing hallucinations of your dead lover everywhere you turn," Warrick said. "If that's not Fey's, then what the hell is it?"

Nax didn't answer.

Warrick looked at him and held out his hands expectantly.

"I am fully aware of my current mental state," Nax said. "I know what is real and what isn't."

"That isn't a reassuring statement."

"I know that I'm not actually seeing Grace," Nax said.

"That doesn't help your case either."

"Then I'm not entirely certain what you want to hear from me."

"Well, to be honest," Warrick said. "Neither am I. I think, though, for starters, I might like to hear that when we get back to the ship you're going to tell the captain and Rabkin about Fey's Euphoria."

"That," Nax said firmly, "is definitely not going to happen. And for that matter, you are not going to bring it to their attention either."

Warrick raised both of his eyebrows.

"You swore an oath," Nax reminded him.

"Your personal well-being supersedes that oath," Warrick said.

"As a matter of fact, it doesn't."

Warrick grumbled something in Vulderran under his breath and turned back to the main engine coils. He slammed all six panels closed a little more violently than necessary.

Warrick glared at Nax, but he didn't say anything else. Instead he walked back around the main engine coils. "Alright," he said to Askon. "What have we got?"

Askon looked up from his console and shook his head. "Nothing."

"What do you mean nothing?" Warrick asked. He glanced back at the engine coils. "Those were six solid gel packs. That should have been more than enough to at least get the main interface up."

Askon wordlessly gestured to the blank console.

Warrick frowned and walked over to his workbag. He took out the datapad he had been using as their map and opened the side panel of Askon's console, yanking out a series of luminescent wires. After studying them for a moment, he separated them into three groups. He took the wires of the smallest group and connected them to his datapad.

A moment later the pad lit up with diagnostics.

Warrick muttered another Vulderran curse.

"What is it?" Nax asked.

Warrick looked up from the datapad and waved a hand around the engineering department. "It's not just this mess. They restructured the entire power grid. Everything's powered into a closed off circuit. All the power'll just go around in circles, never reaching anything else in the ship. Somebody really went out of their way to make sure this ship wasn't going to be used any time soon."

"Fascinating," Askon said.

"Sure," Warrick said. "If you think it's fascinating to get Fim'ai hemorrhoids."

Askon's antenna dipped forward. "I'm afraid I'm not familiar with that reference."

Warrick held up his hand, his finger and thumb about half an inch apart. "They're boils that you can get on your ass if you eat too many of the berries they grow out there. Every time you sit down, they pop and the oils contribute to more boils on your ass."

Askon grimaced in disgust. "No, I'm afraid I do not find that fascinating."

Warrick turned back to his datapad. "Yeah, I didn't think you would. That's basically what we have here."

"I find that analogy to be a bit of a stretch," Askon said.

Warrick made a couple of adjustments on the datapad. "There's really only one way to get the main power up on this old bird: Shut off the circuit."

Askon antennae bent and swayed. "That seems suspiciously easy."

"It's not," Warrick said. "In order to do that, we basically need to shut down all the power on the ship and then restart it. That would effectively wipe out the previous commands and restore all main power. But *everything* would need to be shut down."

"Including life support systems," Nax added.

Warrick nodded, a grim expression on his face. "And it goes without saying that shutting off life support around here is only going to create a whole new set of problems for us since none of us can survive very long without the basics. You know, oxygen. Artificial gravity. That sort of thing."

"That doesn't sound ideal," Askon agreed.

"How long would it take?" Nax asked.

Warrick exhaled, puffing out his cheeks as he ran the numbers through his head. "Ballpark figure? Twenty minutes. Maybe less, maybe more. Honestly, they did a number on this ship. Whoever was flying this old girl really didn't want anybody messing around with it after they were gone. For all we know, I could power everything down and I wouldn't be able to get anything powered back up." Warrick turned off his datapad. "So until we can get a full engineering complement over here, I don't think there's much I'm going to be able to do."

"What about the section rest of the away team is investigating?" Nax asked.

"It's on its own independent power grid," Warrick said. "Or possibly a decentralized generator. Either way, it's definitely running separate from the rest of the ship."

"Perhaps, then, we don't need to shut anything down," Askon said.

"I beg your pardon?" Warrick asked.

Askon took the datapad from Warrick and turned it back on. "A generator seems highly unlikely, especially given the age of this vessel. What is more likely is that the room is still connected to the ship's main power grid, but kept in a walled-off system."

"Doesn't change the facts," Warrick said.

"Actually," Askon said, his slim fingers dancing across the datapad in a nimble fashion, "it does. Using the systems in that room, we might be able to spoof the ship's main computers into thinking we shut everything down." He looked up at Warrick and Nax, his antennae perking straight up. "Thus, achieving the desired results without actually endangering any of us."

There was a loud clunk in the main engine coils and the ship shuddered.

Warrick raised an eyebrow. "You were saying?"

Askon opened his mouth, but before he could say anything the entire room was flooded with light. Around them the consoles started powering up in a familiar cacophony of ancient equipment being used for the first time in centuries.

A thrumming from the main engine coils threatened to overpower the rest of the noise, but it quickly faded away. Dark green energy pulsed through the engine coils down into the electrical system located beneath the floor plates.

On the far side of the room a console exploded into sparks as it powered up, but it was an outlier among the rest of engineering.

Over unseen speakers a voice with a thick accent began speaking. It was clearly a prerecorded message, most likely even older than the ship itself. None of the away team could make out what it was saying, although the structure of its sentences had the familiarity of a safety alert. The announcement ended as a handful of sparks flew off the main engine coils.

Warrick looked at the console next to them as it came to life. Information in a language that seemed vaguely familiar to him started streaming across the screens. "Well I'll be a Chaverus weasel. That actually worked."

Askon's antennae dipped forward. "Thank you."

"You outta check in with Keane," Warrick said, trying to make sense of the data on the console. "Make sure we didn't leave them in the dark up there. Although, according to this, they should be okay."

Nax nodded and tapped his earpiece. "Nax to Commander Keane?"

There was some mild interference for a moment and then screams.

24

"WE HAVE NO NAME FOR IT," the holographic man said. "It has presented no name. It is simply an alien entity that has consumed every inch of our galaxy, of our *universe*. Every being, every creature, every planet, every star...There is nothing left. An entire reality is gone."

He paused, struggling to compose himself.

Dheer and Keane looked at each other, both thinking the same thing, but neither one wanting to say it out loud.

The holographic man took a stuttering breath and then continued, "Our only hope is that by escaping through their network, we may come across another reality, untouched by the darkness." He paused a moment. "We began this journey thirty years ago and we have yet to find one such reality. It would seem that this...darkness has consumed everything. We may be all that's left not only of our universe, but all the others."

The hologram flickered for a moment. Now the man appeared to be older than he had a second ago. His hair was grayer, his face was more haggard and wrinkled. His shoulders slumped forward as he stood.

"It appears we have a…stowaway." He laughed bitterly. "Nearly fifty years and we suspected nothing. It destroyed everything we knew and for fifty years it was hidden beneath our very feet.

"Yesterday the entity made its presence known. We lost nearly a third of our crew. No one knows why it took nearly fifty years. It's not behaving as it had before. There's something…sickly about this one.

"Despite its current state, we cannot seem to kill it. We are unable to determine what has caused its deterioration. It is simply *sick*." He paused. "We are not certain what to do with it. Although we have yet to discover another reality untainted by the darkness, we don't feel comfortable simply casting it aside.

"Working from some early theories from before our universe was consumed, we have been able to construct a cage of sorts for it. The resonance of the magnetic field seems to render it…" He paused again, "Inert, for lack of a better word. We have constructed the field so that it remains independent of our main power source. Eventually our engines will go cold and should we ever find a place that is devoid of the darkness, I'll not be responsible for condemning an entire reality to death."

Suddenly the holographic man disappeared.

A second later, the room went completely dark.

"What happened?" Dheer asked. "Did we trigger something?"

"Hang on," Grell said, tapping at the console, but it wouldn't respond.

Keane flicked on his flashlight, aiming the beam towards the floating silver ball in the center of the room. It seemed unaffected by the sudden power outage.

Dheer adjusted her scanner towards the floating silver object.

"Anything?" Keane asked.

She shook her head. "It's like it's not even there."

"That's not reassuring," he said.

Dheer closed her scanner. "There's only one thing I know of that matches his description." She nodded in the direction of where the holographic man had been.

"What are the odds that the Unity exists in a parallel dimension?" Keane said.

"From where I'm standing? Pretty damn good," Dheer said, eyeing the floating silver ball. "I don't know what the hell is going on here and right now I don't really care. We should get out of here *now*."

"No argument there," Keane said. He nodded at Grell. "Let's go."

Just as suddenly, the power came back on.

"What did you do?" Keane asked.

Grell held up his hands and took a step back from the console. "Nothing. I still don't know what happened."

"Maybe Warrick had something to do with it," Dheer said, reaching for her earpiece.

The hologram reappeared, once again speaking a language they weren't familiar with. This time, it didn't cycle back through to Earth Standard. The expression on the hologram's face was severe.

An alarm started to go off.

"That can't be good," Keane said, looking around for the source of the alarm.

"The magnetic field is going down," Grell said, reaching for his fusion pistol.

The hazy field that had surrounded the floating ball flickered and then disappeared. Without the magnetic field in place, the silver tint of the ball turned black as it dropped to the ground.

Both Keane and Dheer recognized the slick, oily

surface of the ball as it dropped, contorting itself like a glob of liquid that was suddenly free of the limitations of gravity. They immediately took a step back. Keane drew his fusion pistol, switching it to the highest setting.

But it was too late.

The ball struck the floor with a sickening splat. Upon impact gooey tendrils extended from the ball, spreading across the room with lightning speed.

Keane tried to shout out a warning, but before he could even get his mouth open, one of the tendrils lanced itself through Grell's head, right between the eyes.

The final look on Grell's face was that of shock and horror as the back of his head exploded as the tendril made its way through. It expanded into an oily mess of a spider's web and doubled back on to Grell's head, quickly consuming it as it moved down the rest of his body until all that was a left was an oily black mass that bore only a passing resemblance to Grell.

"*Move!*" Keane shouted, pushing Dheer back towards the exit.

The black mass that used to be Grell broke down into a wave and swept across the consoles until it joined the writhing ball in the center of the room.

Keane's leg screamed at him as he dropped the cane and pushed his muscles past limits they weren't ready to exceed. He gritted his teeth together to keep from shouting in pain and instead tried to focus on getting Dheer out of there alive and in one piece.

Two more tendrils lashed out towards Dheer and Keane as they raced back towards the exit. Instead of striking them, the tendrils slammed into the stacks of skulls and the long dead heads went flying around them.

Keane fired at the black mass over his shoulder.

The first shot went nowhere and more tendrils spread

out from the black mass, whipping their way across the room like a blind man looking for his closest support.

However, Keane got lucky with the second shot. It hit the crystal lens of the magnetic field generator. The explosion was small, but the gravity in the room momentarily shifted as it went off.

Suddenly the black tendrils were untethered from everything. There was a haunting, inhuman scream from the black mass as it was momentarily caught in the small gravity well of the explosion.

Dheer started to topple under the shift in the gravity, but Keane caught her and shoved her the last few feet out into the main hallway.

The advantage of the brief explosion was small and lasted for less than a few seconds. Had Keane not been nursing a leg injury, he most likely would have made it out to the relative safety of the main corridor with Dheer

But he didn't.

Gravity quickly restored itself and Keane's knee chose that moment to give up.

He nearly dropped to the ground as the black mass screamed again. Keane grabbed a stack of skulls to steady him.

The tendrils lurched back towards the black mass and then just as quickly exploded across the room.

Keane tightened his grip on his pistol and made a mad dash for the door.

But his leg wouldn't cooperate any longer.

The oily darkness rained down around him, sharpening itself to razor point edges. One sliced straight through Keane's left arm.

Keane couldn't stop himself from screaming this time.

He stared numbly at the fusion pistol as it fell to the

ground, still in the grip of his left hand, his brain not quite making the necessary connection.

Keane stumbled to his feet, oblivious to the shattered skulls that were falling around him. He reached for his left arm, but couldn't find it. He glanced down at the bloody stump that used to be his left arm and missed another tendril as it pierced his left leg.

Keane screamed again, dropping to the ground, surrounded by a pile of broken skulls and a growing pool of his own blood.

Keane felt his body lurch as something yanked him back towards the black mass and in that moment he knew that he was going to die.

25

Dheer watched in horror as the black mass cut Keane's arm off.

Her mind raced for some kind of solution as Keane went down, a dazed and numb look in his eyes that she had seen too many times in patients who knew they weren't going to make it.

More black tendrils spread out across the room. Slithering and speeding their way through the skulls.

Dheer pulled out her fusion pistol, fumbling with it for a second.

Keane screamed as the black mass speared his left leg and went down.

Dheer quickly disabled the safeties on the pistol and set it to overload. She raced back into the room, tossing the pistol into the black mass.

Seconds ticked by as Dheer dropped to the ground, sliding across the floor and snatching up Keane's pistol from the clutch of his ruined left hand. With her other hand she grabbed his right arm and pulled back against the tendril that was dragging him back towards the black mass.

The tendril in his leg burst all the way through. It was a thin spear that quickly expanded and separated into three anchors that latched themselves onto Keane's leg.

The black mass pulled harder and Dheer felt him slipping from her grip.

She tried to remember how much time she had, but all she could focus on was Keane's hand slipping away from her.

Dheer whipped the pistol around and fired off several shots at the tendril dragging him back. One of them struck and the oily black cord exploded, splattering across the floor.

Keane looked at her dumbly. His eyes were vacant. She wasn't even sure he was seeing her.

Dheer jumped to her feet, pulling him towards the exit as more tendrils raced across the room.

The exit was only a few feet away, but the darkness rained down all around them. Thick, oily barriers dropping from the ceiling with heavy *thuds,* crushing the skulls into a fine powder that disappeared into the oily darkness.

They weren't going to make it.

Then her pistol detonated.

The black mass screamed again under the pain of the explosion.

Dheer tightened her grip on Keane and raced for the doorway as the black tendrils dissolved into puddles around them.

The black mass screamed and thrashed around. Black strands momentarily strengthened and thickened, sharpening to razor sharp edges, before abruptly fading away back to formless liquid.

Dheer heaved with all her strength and tossed Keane

out into the corridor. She turned and fired at the locking mechanism Keane had so carefully manipulated before. Immediately the doors slammed shut.

Dheer scrambled, placing herself between Keane and the room, holding the pistol with both hands, waiting to see if the black mass was going to break through.

She could hear it screaming and wailing on the other side of the door. She could feel it thrashing about violently as the flooring beneath her rattled.

And then there was nothing.

No noise. No movement.

Nothing.

Dheer waited.

Distantly, she heard alarms going off.

Sweat dripped into her eyes.

Behind her Keane coughed and groaned.

She glanced back at him, focusing on the gaping wound at his shoulder and the black spear that was still attached to his leg. She thought of the hike back to the shuttle. She tried to calculate how much blood he had already lost and how much more he would lose before they would make it back to the shuttle. And despite herself, she found herself calculating the odds of his survival.

Out of the corner of her eye, she spotted something on the ground, leaking from under the door. In the darkness she couldn't tell if it was Keane's red blood or something else.

26

NOISE EXPLODED AROUND THEM.

Alarms blared.

Multiple voices talked over each other in a multitude of languages.

Nax felt a sharp stab of urgency in his chest and he started for the exit.

Warrick grabbed his shoulder. "Where the hell do you think you're going?"

"The rest of the away team is in danger," Nax said, yanking his shoulder out of Warrick's grip.

"And what the hell are you going to do?" Warrick asked. "We can't get to them," He held up the datapad for Nax to see. "What the hell do you think all these alarms are for? Half the ship just *decompressed*. You won't make it. Hell, I don't think *we're* going to make it."

"I cannot…" Nax trailed off. His breathing became labored. His pupils dilated.

All around them, Nax kept seeing Grace.

He blinked, trying to pull his focus from the ghostly visages of his former love. But she wouldn't go away.

"*Nax-*," An explosion on the other side of the main engine coils cut Warrick off.

The ship shook violently as smoke poured out of the overhead panels in a shower of sparks.

Abruptly all the voices blasting over the speakers went silent.

"That can't be good," Warrick said.

A new alarm started blaring.

"That's definitely not good," Warrick added.

The ship shuddered and the floor shifted beneath them as the artificial gravity fought to compensate for parts of the ship that were suddenly bending opposite directions.

A loud groaning noise was preceded by a pylon crashing through overhead bulkheads.

Warrick tried to push Nax clear of the falling debris, but the metal shrapnel was raining down everywhere, cutting across their uniforms. Another violent shudder rolled through the ship and they both dropped to the ground.

"Shit!" Warrick exclaimed. He looked at Nax. "Are you okay?"

Nax just waved his concerns away. The pain from the cuts focused him for the moment and the images of Grace seemed to have disappeared.

"We're moving!" Askon shouted, gripping the wall for support.

Warrick glanced back at him. "What the hell are you talking about?"

Askon gestured to the main engine coils. A pulse was running through them as a familiar sound reached Warrick's ears over the new alarm.

"The hell?" Warrick said. He stumbled over to the console as engineering rattled apart around him. "How the hell are we *moving*?"

Askon shook his head and tightened his grip on the wall. "Possibly some kind of preset subroutine that was activated once we restored power?"

Warrick worked over the console, attempting to shut down the engines, but nothing responded. He pounded his fists against the console in frustration. "Son of a bitch! The damn system won't even tell me where we're going."

New alarms went off as the ship shook violently around them.

Distantly, Warrick heard more explosions from the decks above them.

"Nax!" Warrick barked over his shoulder. When the helmsman didn't respond, Warrick looked around for him.

He found Nax on his knees, staring up at a plume of smoke, a distant look in his eyes.

"Bloody hell," Warrick muttered. "I don't have time for this."

There was another explosion and half the consoles in engineering went dark.

"Commander?" Askon said. The look on his face asked the rest of the unspoken question.

"I don't know," Warrick replied. "I'd like to say that I'm working on a plan, but now I don't know if we can even get out of this damn room."

Warrick stumbled back over to Nax. Two steps in and he felt like he was trying to walk with two fifty pound weights strapped to his back. The artificial gravity was close to failing. Warrick took a deep breath and tried to push through it. Just as suddenly, the extra weight disappeared and he was abruptly running across engineering. Unprepared for the sudden shifts in gravity, he tripped, dropping to the ground in front of Nax.

"Nax!"

Nax didn't respond. He kept staring off into the smoke. His lips moved, but no words came out.

Warrick gripped the Natuzzi's shoulders and shook him. "Nax! Snap out of it, you orange bastard!"

Nax blinked and he looked at Warrick as if noticing him for the first time. "Warrick?"

"Hey there, welcome back," Warrick said with a grim smile.

Nax took a deep, shuddering breath. "Forgive me."

A power conduit exploded above them raining sparks down across engineering, setting off a handful of fires.

Warrick flinched, raising his arm to shield his face from the sparks. "Consider yourself forgiven. I'd push the issue and tell you to talk to Rabkin as soon as we get back to the ship, but I don't think that's going to happen."

The pulse in the main engine coils sped up, although there was no discernible increase in the ship's speed. The floor paneling beneath them shuddered and erupted.

Nax and Warrick leapt to their feet, jumping away from a spot that was quickly turning into a sinkhole.

"What is going on?" Nax asked.

Warrick shook his head. "Ship's falling apart."

"Why?"

"Probably because it's too damn old."

"I'm not certain that's the only reason," Askon said. He made his way over to them and held up Warrick's datapad.

On the map of the ship, there was an unidentified object that was moving rapidly through the vessel with very little regard for things such as walls or structural integrity.

"What the hell is that?" Warrick asked.

Nax noted the path of the object. "That is most likely the cause of our teammates' distress." He tapped his earpiece. "Nax to Keane?"

There was no response.

Nax looked at Warrick, who just shook his head.

"There's no way we can make it up there," Warrick said.

"We might not have to," Askon said, gesturing to the current path of the object on the map. "Whatever it is, its clearly headed our way."

27

"SOMEBODY TELL me what the hell is going on?" Mitchell barked, storming onto the bridge. Rabkin and Calloway followed close behind.

Steve was already there, lazily slouched in the captain's chair. He gave Calloway an intense stink-eye as she walked past him towards her console.

"Massive power surges coming from the *Eternal Hand of God*," Sadler said from her console. "It looks like the main engine core is going into meltdown. We're looking at detonation within five to eight minutes."

"Mother of God," Rabkin whispered, looking at the viewscreen in horror. "What happened?"

"We don't know," Sadler said. "We lost contact with the away team."

"What was the last we heard?" Mitchell asked.

"They were in the process of restoring main power and Dheer and Keane had discovered the source of the distress signal."

Mitchell glared at Steve. "Get out of my damn chair."

Steve hopped to his feet. "Sorry. Didn't realize you were territorial about it."

"Is our signal being jammed?" Mitchell asked, sitting down.

Sadler shook her head. "Honestly? I don't know, sir. We just…can't reach them." She took a deep breath. "That's not all."

"What the hell else could you possibly have to tell us?" Rabkin grumbled.

"The ship started moving."

"*Moving*? Where the hell is it going?"

"Based on the telemetry? Back towards the entrance to the wormhole," Sadler said. "I had helm match speed."

Mitchell turned to Steve who was strolling around the bridge, his hands behind his back, whistling. He paused and met Mitchell's gaze. "Told you so."

"You knew this was going to happen," Mitchell said.

"Well, I didn't warn you to get your people off there because I thought one of them was going to get a nasty paper cut," Steve replied.

Mitchell shook his head. "No, it's more than that. Back in my quarters-"

"Careful, Captain," Steve interrupted, glancing around the bridge. "People might *talk*."

Mitchell glared at him. "You said that time was like an open book to you. You knew *this* was going to happen."

Steve held a hand to his mouth in mock surprise. "So you were paying attention. I must say, Captain, I never suspected a *thing*." He gave Mitchell a slow clap. "Well played. Well played."

"What's going on?" Mitchell asked.

"You mean, other than the fact that you're kicking yourself for not listening to me earlier?" Steve said. "It's a failsafe. The previous occupants of that ship were all too aware of what the Unity was capable of and should anyone be foolish enough to go poking around their ship long after they were gone, they set everything to blow. Of course, as I understood it, the ship was supposed to make its way back to the Network first." He tilted his head to the side, watching as the *Eternal Hand of God* slowly made its way across space. "I don't think it's going to make it, though."

Mitchell turned his chair away from Steve. "What are our options, people?"

"Options, Captain?" Sadler said.

"I'm not about to leave our people over there to die," Mitchell said.

"To be fair," Steve said, "you don't know that they already aren't."

"Shut up," Mitchell snapped at him.

"Captain, the energy readings on the vessel just spiked dramatically," Sadler said. "I don't think we have any options. At this distance, even with our deflectors at full, I don't think the *Defiance* could survive that explosion unscathed."

Mitchell pressed his hands against the armrests of his chair, fighting the urge to snap at his crew. He stared at the ship on the screen, watching as small explosions broke out across its surface.

A proximity alarm started to go off.

Rabkin stepped down next to Mitchell's command. "Gavin," he said quietly.

Mitchell cut him off with a raise of his hand and turned to face Steve again. Mitchell pointed at him. "You can get them off."

Steve looked at him with the sincerity of a man who hadn't even noticed anyone was paying attention to him. "I beg your pardon?"

Mitchell got up from his seat. "You can get my people off that ship."

Steve looked at the vessel on the viewscreen, nodding his head. "Well, yes, I suppose I could."

Tense seconds ticked by as no one said anything.

Mitchell walked up to him until their faces were less than an inch apart. "What the hell then?"

Steve made a face and took a step back. "I'm afraid you're going to have to be a little more specific, Mitch."

"Get my people off that ship."

Steve thought about it for a moment and shook his head. "No, I don't think so. For starters, I'm not one of your crew. You can't exactly go barking orders at me. I mean, technically, you *can*. Because, obviously, you just *did*. But it wouldn't exactly be a great use of your time."

"You *have* to get them off."

"I don't *have* to do anything, Captain. To me, you're like simple, half thought out scribbles on a discarded napkin. Can you imagine a doodle telling you that you *have* to do something?"

"This is *bullshit*," Rabkin growled. "Ever since you got here you've been telling us to get off that ship."

Steve nodded enthusiastically. "I *know*. I *warned* you and I *warned* you." He held out his hands, his fingers bent at the knuckles. "But you wouldn't *listen*." Steve clapped his hands together. "And now here we are. Think about all the headache you would have saved yourselves if you had just *listened* to me. Think about Lieutenant Commander Keane and all the *limbs* that he would have saved if you had *listened* to me. Life, in general, would be better for everyone in this universe, if you had just *listened to me*."

"Captain," Sadler said, her voice broaching on frantic. "The main core is approaching critical mass. Less than three minutes until total detonation. If we don't move the *Defiance* now…"

On the screen, larger explosions were breaking out along the length of the *Eternal Hand of God*.

Steve's eyes widened, watching the ship slowly break apart. "I certainly hope none of your people were in any of those sections. It'd be a hell of a way to go. I mean, it's better than getting eaten by the Unity. But I don't think anyone has 'getting sucked out into the vacuum of space' near the top of their Ideal Ways to Die."

"What do you want from me?" Mitchell snapped. "Do you want me to beg?"

"Beg? Don't be so pedantic." Steve leaned forward and tapped Mitchell's temple. "I want you to *think*."

"Think about *what?*" Mitchell said through gritted teeth.

Steve pointed to the viewscreen. "Before this is over the Unity is going to take a lot more than just a handful of your favorite crewmen. One day that's going to be *your* ship out there. Because that's how everything *ends*. This isn't the first ship to momentarily escape the Unity and it won't be the last. When they ran, there wasn't anything *left*. They were, quite literally, the absolute last beings in their entire universe. Septentrigintillions upon septentrigintillions and all that was left in the end were a few thousand souls. No one *thought*. No one took a moment to accept what was coming. They just ran around like chickens with their damn heads cut off for a couple of hundred years as the Unity ate them up one by one, until all that was left was one ship with a couple thousand frantic beings who never thought it would come to *this*."

Steve took a step forward, towering over Mitchell. "Tell me, Captain Gavin Mitchell, does that really sound like an ideal way to end your existence? To close out the chapter of an entire reality?"

No one spoke on the bridge.

Precious seconds ticked by.

Finally Mitchell turned away from him and sat back down in his command chair. "What are our options?"

Sadler looked at Steve and then back at Mitchell. "Sir?"

"We've got less than three minutes before that ship out there blows up," Mitchell said, focusing on the viewscreen. "I want to hear options."

Sadler stared blankly at her console. "I...don't think we have any."

Steve stepped in front of Mitchell, waving a hand. "Hello. Did you forget about me?"

Mitchell didn't look at him. "You've made your position clear."

"Based on your behavior here, I don't think I have," Steve said. "Do I need to use smaller words? Draw you a picture? Sing you a damn song?"

"Get the hell off my damn ship," Mitchell said.

Steve shook his head. "You genuinely can't see it, can you? You've already *lost*. Did you not hear me when I said the Unity has already infected Earth? You lost this fight before it ever began. You lost this battle before the Unity ever arrived here. It's *over*. You're worried about losing a handful of crewmen? You've lost entire civilizations and you don't know it yet."

Mitchell glared at him. "You don't get to say that. I don't know who the hell you think you are, but you don't get to say that. Nothing's over. Not as long there's at least one of us still alive and kicking, it's not over. So unless you plan on offering some real help around here, get off my ship."

Steve paused for a moment, watching Mitchell carefully. Behind him the *Eternal Hand of God* began to break apart.

"Oh, you're a real piece of work, aren't you, Mitch?" Steve said.

Calloway gasped as the forward section of the ship disappeared into explosions.

"Alright then," Steve snapped his fingers.

Instantly Dheer and Keane appeared at the rear section of the bridge, right in front of Calloway.

Calloway screamed, jolting out of her seat at the sudden sight of them.

Dheer was bent over Keane's ruined form, her hands pressed over the bloody stump that used to be Keane's left arm. She was desperately trying to stop the flow of blood with nothing but her bare hands, completely unaware in the change of her location.

Rabkin rushed forward. "Get me an emergency medical team up here now!"

At the sound of Rabkin's voice, Dheer looked up with a numb expression of surprise. "What the hell?" she mumbled.

Keane's eyes rolled back in his head as he coughed up more blood. His body began to spasm violently, splattering blood across the bridge.

Calloway screamed again and somebody pulled her to a rear corner of the bridge away from the scene.

Steve cleared his throat, bringing Mitchell's attention back to him. "Just for the record, all you really had to do was say 'Please.'" He snapped his fingers again.

This time Nax, Warrick and Askon appeared behind him, looking dazed and confused.

On the viewscreen, the *Eternal Hand of God* erupted as the main core reached critical mass. Proximity alarms screamed as the explosion threatened to engulf the *Defiance*.

Mitchell jumped out of his seat. "Helm, get us-!"

"And now, Captain, we do it the hard way." Steve snapped his fingers for a third and final time and in an instant, Steve and Captain Gavin Mitchell simply disappeared.

TO BE CONTINUED IN:
ACT OF GOD
Available Now

_Subscribe to my newsletter and I'll let you know as soon as the next
Defiance book is ready to read._

Sign Up Here

https://onestrayword.beehiiv.com/subscribe

ABOUT THE AUTHOR

Jason Krumbine loves to write! He's happily married and lives in Orlando, FL where he enjoys visiting Disney World with his daughter and wife.

If you want to get an automatic email when Jason's next book is released sign up here https://onestrayword.beehiiv.com/subscribe Your email address will never be shared and you can unsubscribe at any time.

Stop By and Say Hi!

You can connect with Jason at either his website, www.jasonkrumbine.com, Facebook, Twitter (@jasonkrumbine) or good ole' fashion email onestrayword@jasonkrumbine.com. He's always up for a talk about the newest Star Trek movie or what's happening in the world of comic books and TV.

ALSO BY JASON KRUMBINE

Defiance (Book 1)

Hand of God (Book 2)

Act of God (Book 3)

The Test of Truth (Book 4)

The Price of Paradise (Book 5)

The Value of Terror (Book 6)

———————

Reapers in Heels

One Stiletto in the Grave (Book 1)

Death Wears Stilettos (Book 2)

A Grave Full of Stilettos (Book 3)

———————

Star Girl

Dating the Villain (Book 1)

Dating the Hero (Book 2)

Dating Disaster (Book 3)

———————

The Castle Sisters

<u>*Volume One – The Impossible Darkness*</u>

The Impossible Rescue (Book 1)

The Arctic Isle of Doom (Book 2)

The Invasion of the Imaginary Friends (Book 3)

The Mall of Eternity (Book 4)

The Doomsday Event (Book 5)

———————

Cupid's Daughter

Learning to Love (Book 1)

Looking for Love (Book 2)

Rupert & Me

Tales From Under the Desk

Holy Words from Under Desk

Dear Rupert

Seeking a Few Good Minions

Other Books

Heaven's Superhero: The Third Creation

Explorers of the Unknown

Outlawed Love

A Graveyard Romance

Cupid's Daughter

The Grym Brothers